Tales From Beyond the Veil

E.B. Hunter

Published by Heorot Press, 2024.

This is a work of fiction. Similarities to real people, places, or events are entirely coincidental.

TALES FROM BEYOND THE VEIL

First edition. January 15, 2024.

ISBN: 979-8223957775

Written by E.B. Hunter.

Table of Contents

To everyone who took a chance.

Thank you.

Graveyard Shift

———

I'd never felt particularly worthy of anything, but I had always aspired to be more. I'd never had much going for me, and I guess it would have been safer, much safer, had it stayed that way. I just felt like I deserved more, ya know?

On the night that changed my life, I was feeling extremely disparaged by my circumstance. I'd quit at the Gas N' Gulp the week before, after I landed this great marketing job in Madison (full dental and everything). Things were looking up. It took three days for my life to go from happiness to total despair, and I found myself back at the Gas N' Gulp working my old graveyard shift.

I felt I deserved the job–I had the schooling after all–but it turns out some Ivy Leaguer wunderkind came available, and it left me out on my community college ass. I'm lucky Melissa didn't leave right then. Don't feel too bad though, they told me they'd, 'call if anything came up'.

The bell on the door clinked and I looked up to see what fresh hell was coming for me. My manager, Martin, held the door open. The wind assaulted my skin, sending goosebumps up my arms and letting flakes rush in around him.

"I'm off for the night, Alex. Do you need anything before I go?" he said.

"No, I'm all set here. Just close that door would ya? That wind is freezing tonight."

He dipped his head, his long beard touching his chest, and turned to go, waving behind him. Once the tail lights on his '98 Toyota were swallowed by the blizzard, I went to the docking station, plugged in, and cranked some Modest Mouse to get me through the next three minutes and forty four seconds.

Ian Brock was in full form when the bells chimed again and a lady older than my grandmother shuffled in. She was hunched over a wooden cane and wore layer after layer of shawls with little shimmering trinkets poking out from the folds on each one, making her unsteady gait sound like Tinker Bell was dancing somewhere in the folds.

I watched her as she shuffled up to the counter, wondering all the while, *hasn't this woman ever heard of a parka?* She looked up at me once she made it to the counter, and her wide, pale blue eyes stared directly into mine. "What can I do for you?" I asked.

"Package of Camels."

I grabbed the cigarettes from under the counter. When I looked back down at the woman, her eyes had narrowed and her mouth was turned in a grim look of satisfaction.

What the hell is up with this lady? I thought while saying, "That's six eighty five."

"May I ask you a question?" she asked, making no move to pay.

"Uh-I guess..." I said. *What could she want?*

"Are you happy?"

"Happy?"

"Yes. Do you feel satisfied?"

Her smile grew wider and under the fluorescent lights, it looked twisted. I thought it would wrap itself all the way around her head. "I work at a gas station, it's midnight, and my shift only started an hour ago. What do you think?"

Normally I wouldn't be so rude to what seemed like a sweet old lady, but her face kept moving in weird directions, her lips looking full, then thin and her eyes turned from hooded to bugged out. It was like she wore several different faces at once and they were fighting for control.

I pushed my glasses up and rubbed my eyes, sure I'd finally lost it, but when I looked back down, her face was still and she was holding out a crumpled twenty.

"You alright?" she asked, her voice dripped honey.

"I–I'm fine." I said. I grabbed the bill and made her change.

"What would you say if I gave you the chance to take everything you ever wanted?"

"I would say the world doesn't work like that. That I wouldn't be able to take anything, because people would stop me. They have an order to things."

"What if I told you I could change that? Disrupt the order and allow you to have real success?"

"I'd like to see that. I could use a win." I took my glasses off to clean them, my eyes felt like I had just stared at one of those 3D pictures for too long.

"Alright, it's a deal."

"Deal? What deal?" I said, putting my glasses back on to see the lady had disappeared. I leaned over the counter to see if she had bent to get a candy bar or something, but she wasn't there. The bell hadn't jingled, and the wind never blew in from the storm. She was just gone.

"I'm losing my *fucking* mind." I cursed, rubbing my eyes again, and putting more fingerprints on my freshly cleaned lenses.

The bell rang, and my hands shot down from my eyes to see if the old bitch was making a run for it, but it wasn't her. Just Mike coming in before his shift at the power plant.

"Alex! You're back?" he said.

"Did a lady walk by you on your way in?"

"Uh–no. What kind of lady?"

"She was really short, and had like a bunch of shawls all over her."

Mike raised his eyebrows and puffed out his cheeks,

"Little wooden cane?" I said, "No?"

"Sorry buddy. No one out there but me and Jack Frost."

Melissa's right, I need to cut back on the caffeine. I watched Mike head back to the coffee station, grabbing a snowball from the shelf without breaking stride.

"So, why're you back? I thought you were, 'rid of this place forever.'"

"Yeah, well, things didn't go like I planned."

"What happened?"

"They hired some kid who went to Princeton and has a better complexion."

"Typical. Fucking assholes." Mike shook his head, placing his goods on the counter. "I thought you had a contract?"

"I was supposed to sign my first day."

"Motherfuckers."

"Yeah; so I'm back."

"Well, lucky Mahir took you back." he said, using Martin's real name. Mike refused to call him Martin saying, *what's so Goddamned hard about saying Mahir?*

"Yeah. That's me. Alex 'Lucky' Rodrigo."

"Come on man. Know what you have here, cause there ain't no jobs out there. I'm lucky I'm union."

I laughed, "Rub it in."

"Every chance I get." He pulled some money from his jacket and counted out some small bills.

"Hey, check this for me too, would you?" he said, setting down a crumpled lotto ticket.

I picked up the ticket and glanced at the front. It looked more or less normal, but the lettering was red where Mike had signed. So were his numbers:

04 25 14 09 26 89 7

His little girl's and his wife's birth dates, his old stand by numbers he played every week, with a 7 for good luck.

"Mike, you know they won't take this if it's in red pen."

"What's in red pen?"

"The lotto, it's signed in red." I held the ticket for him to look at.

"I think you need to take the night off, man. That's in black ink."

"What? No, it's in re–" I looked back down at the ticket and the whole thing had turned crimson, staining my fingertips red. I blinked hard and rubbed my fingers together, but they felt normal, not slippery with what I felt certain was blood. "Sorry," I said, "I must be losin' it." and flashed Mike a smile.

"All good, man." he chuckled. "Give it a check for me, maybe I won big and can get you some therapy."

My hands were shaking now, and the ticket was still red. I passed the barcode under the scanner and the machine binged, singing out that the ticket was a winner.

Mike jumped up and down, hopping from foot to foot and rubbing his hands together, "Hoo doggy! I knew it was only a matter of time. How much'd I win?"

I looked at the little screen with the flashing lights reading 'grand prize winner' over and over, then looked at the sign hanging above me that read the total. "All of it. Mike, you won the jackpot!"

"What!?" he shouted before doing several fist pumps in the air. "The whole thing?"

"Don't get excited yet," I said, "better take it to the Lottery Commission and verify it first." I had almost forgotten the red that was dripping from the ticket and onto my hands, smearing everything I touched.

"Don't worry, I ain't gonna quit my job tonight. Gotta make sure it's for real!"

Mike kept talking, I knew he had, I could see his lips moving, but I couldn't hear him anymore. I looked behind him and I could see the old lady, she was standing just behind the Lay's chips stand and her face had morphed again, her smile wide enough that it touched her ears and her eyes were bugged out to the point of bursting. Black veins, like burst blood vessels under the skin, stained her lips and eyelids, making her look like walking death.

Mike was still talking, but all I could hear was the woman's voice in my ear. I saw her lips moving from across the store, but her voice paid no heed to physics as I heard her saccharine tone, "Take it. Take the ticket. This is my gift to you. You can make yourself a new man. Maybe Melissa will stick around. Your parents will love you, once you buy them a house. Take the ticket."

"No!" I shouted.

Mike stopped talking and took a step back. He looked from my face and followed my line of sight to the shelves and then back to my eyes. "You alright? Need me to call somebody?"

The thing that had been an old lady smiled wider and laughed, the top of her head moving independently from her jaw in a grotesque show of teeth, blackened lips and tongue. She floated to the ceiling, dissipating into red smoke, and my knees shook.

I turned to Mike, taking my eyes off the smoke and he had his phone held to his ear. I heard a tiny voice on the line say, "911, what's your emergency?" right before the smoke screeched and flew down toward me. It landed at my feet then swirled its way around my body, roiling and prodding along my flesh to find an opening. It crawled up and found my mouth, paralyzed open in a silent scream. Then it found my nose, my eyes, my ears. The smoke forced its way in, choking the air from my lungs, invading my brain, my being.

My body shook, and I could feel my arms jerk around like I was a marionette. They moved separately from my consciousness, and I could feel the old lady taking shape inside of me, telling my body to do what my mind wouldn't.

"Alex, man, stay back!" Mike yelled, his hands held out in front of him. The glow of the phone caught my eye and the woman flung my hand at him, knocking the phone and the little voice across the room to slide under the coolers. *Stop! Get out of me!* I shouted in my own head, hoping the thing would get out of my body.

She hopped me up onto the counter and in one smooth step, I went crashing down on Mike. He was six five, probably weighed 275, and he was a linebacker in highschool. None of that mattered with this thing in the driver's seat.

He fell backward, scrambling to get away. My hands reached out and grabbed him by the throat, crunching his windpipe. He grabbed my forearms, and I cried out to him in my head, *Get me off you! Get this fucking thing off!*, but all Mike heard was my throat growling and grunting as I slammed his head into the industrial linoleum. Again, and again, until he stopped fighting.

My legs turned around and then my shoulders followed, ambling my body back to the counter to grab the ticket.

I fell to my knees as the bitch forced her way out my throat. It felt like razor blades coated in salt and I buckled, falling onto all fours as the last bit of her left me to spew blood onto the ground. The pain in my forearms where Mike had tried to break my hold was unreal, my flesh throbbed with each beat of my heart, and tears streamed down my face. Not for my pain, but because I would rather he broke my arms clean off than have him dead by my hands. I wept for his wife and daughter. What could I tell them? How could anyone explain...this?

"Leave now, or my gift will be wasted." the thing said. I hadn't noticed her standing over me, back to wearing her innocent old lady face. "They will be here soon."

She was right, even in the snowstorm, the cops had made good time, and the sirens blared. Red and blue light bounced off the snow and filled the store making it look like a rave.

"Fuck you and your gift." I spat at her, but more blood choked me, and sent me into a coughing fit.

She laughed, "You didn't want to be here. Now you won't be. I released you."

"You killed me."

"I gave you what you asked for." She faded away, her cackle fading with her and I heard the megaphone.

"Drop the weapon and come out with your hands up!"

I didn't know what he was talking about, I didn't have a weapon. But my hand was suddenly heavy and cool as a black handgun appeared, my fingers wrapped around the grip and trembling.

"I'm so sorry, Mike." I stood up, using the last of my strength to run for the door on legs that shook with each step. I was sure I wouldn't make it to the door, but I deserved what was across that threshold. I knew that. So I forced my body to keep going.

I made it far enough to see the state trooper's stupid fuzzy hat, and then there was a pop.

After that, there was only darkness.

Everglades

———

I had gotten a tea towel from my little boy last Mother's Day. It had pictures of flowers and butterflies with little fairies dancing across it. My husband told me Everett had saved up and paid for it himself, his gap toothed grin beaming as he handed the coins to the clerk.

I never would've thought when I got the towel that I'd be using it to keep the blood inside of his tiny body. That the fairies and the flowers would all become muddled in the dark red as it spilled from his arteries.

His father had been away on a business trip– selling condos in Florida often meant meetings with seniors in New York. We didn't mind though, the money was good, and I worked at the seniors center while Everett went to school. It was a good system, it worked for us. Right up until the day it didn't.

We normally visited a food truck for 'Taco Tuesdays', but I'd had a stressful day and didn't feel up to it. We argued for a bit, but Everett accepted the trade off to order pizza from home.

"It has to be taco pizza though!" He said, and I'd laughed.

"No problem buddy, I know just the place."

Reflecting, I wish we had stuck to tradition. Maybe the burglar would have been gone with only my pearl earrings instead of turning Everett into collateral damage.

I had let him out of the car, and he ran to the house as fast as he could, just like always.

He punched in the code and opened the door, throwing his bag on the floor and bolting up to his room. Just like always.

I stood in the doorway and heard his uncertain voice say, "Mom?" before shouting, "Mom!" and all the hairs on my neck stood. A breeze tickled my skin and I saw the patio door open across from me. I grabbed the mace from my purse, a relic from my youth that I kept just in case, and ran up the stairs two at a time. *Something's wrong, someone's here.*

I made it to the top of the stairs on legs made of jelly and froze when a voice growled, "Stay where you are, bitch."

I saw a man holding Everett at the end of the hall, a knife pressed to his throat.

"Please, don't hurt him." I wanted to shout, but my throat only let me whisper.

"I'm going out the way I came. Back up and don't do anything stupid, and no one gets hurt."

I nodded my compliance.

"Drop the can." he said, and I did.

I walked down the stairs backwards, slow as possible with my hands raised, and the man followed me down and through to the kitchen. He side-stepped around me, backing toward the door and out onto the concrete patio.

I tried to warn him, but my voice caught in my throat, fear freezing my vocal chords. His foot caught the edge of Everett's scooter and sent him sprawling onto the lawn, his blade flashing in the sunlight as he went down.

Everett fell forward and clutched his neck, making a terrible gurgling sound, and the burglar scampered to his feet and ran for the fence.

I fell to my knees beside my boy then brought him into the house, my body moving independently from my mind as I pulled him inside and laid him down on the cool tiled floor. I yanked the towel from the oven door and pressed it on his neck, the blood saturating it. His eyes flickered and all I could smell was pennies.

"Everett! Everett! Stay with me, stay awake!" I screamed and his eyes fluttered.

The bleeding slowed, and I reached for the phone, sitting just out of reach. I let go for a second to snatch the phone, and the blood started pouring again.

I reapplied pressure, and Everett's hands fell from his neck to the floor. His skin almost matched the white ceramic. I don't remember dialing, but I was on with the operator. They didn't get past the opening line of their script before I screamed, "3210 Everglades Boulevard South! I need an ambulance, my son's been cut!"

"Alright ma'am," they replied as if I had ordered coffee, "The ambulance is on the way. I need you to keep pressure on the wound. Where was he cut?"

"His neck," I started to sob, my vision blurring as I switched to speakerphone with my free hand and set the phone down on a bare part of tile, the only small square not covered in blood. "He's been cut on his neck!"

"Is he conscious?"

"No, he–his eyes are closed."

I heard the sirens approach as she said, "A unit is in your area. They're on the way, ma'am. Keep pressure on his neck, but don't press on his windpipe. We need to keep that open."

Oh fuck, I thought and laid my head next to his chest. "He's still breathing, but it's really shallow."

The door was already open, so the paramedics got inside easily to take over. The phone was kicked out of the way and I was left looking at Everett's feet, his torso obscured by the paramedic's wide shoulders, and clutching the bloody tea towel to my chest.

They had him 'stable' and on a gurney within an indeterminate time. I can't tell you if it took an hour or thirty seconds, my mind was too far gone to comprehend what was in front of me.

They loaded him into the ambulance and I jumped into the back, holding his hand the entire way to the hospital as the large paramedic held his neck closed. I think I was crying while we drove, but I was too numb to say for certain. I knew I felt like I should be crying. Like I should be wailing and pulling my hair out, but I couldn't access it. I knew if I went there, I would never come back.

We screeched into Our Lady of Mercy and they unloaded Everett. A woman in a white coat met us at the ambulance and rushed him inside while an administrator asked me questions as we followed.

After filling out the forms and putting down the insurance information, they sent me to a room filled with glossy magazines and short purple chairs to wait.

A man sat there, beneath the flickering fluorescent lights, reading a worn copy of the National Geographic with an alligator on the cover. I remember the cover well because the green tracksuit he was wearing matched the gator perfectly.

I still had the towel, and I sat in one of the purple chairs and stared at it. I had lost all track of my surroundings, my vision focusing on the ruined cloth, staring at it as blood clotted on my hands and in the fibers. I had thought, *why the hell didn't someone take this from me?* When the man spoke and I jumped out of my skin.

"What've you got there?" he asked, his voice a rich tenor. He'd folded the magazine and set it in his lap, leaning toward me with an eyebrow raised.

"I—it was..."

"I think I can see. Someone hurt pretty bad then? Someone you love?"

I couldn't hold back and tears squirted forth as I went from calm to ugly crying in a nanosecond.

The man just nodded and set the magazine on the table. His hair was cut into a tight white afro that contrasted the dark umber of his skin. He was old and wisened and kind as he said, "Do they know if he'll make it? Your little boy?"

I stopped crying and looked at him, "How did you know it was my boy?"

"Fifty-fifty guess. You're cryin' like it's your child in there. It's a different kind of cry. I know." he tapped the side of his nose, his smile fading for only a moment.

I suppose that's true, I thought, nodding and sniffling.

"I can save him."

"What?"

"Your boy. I can make sure he lives."

"What the hell are you talking about? Do you work here, are you some sort of doctor?"

He laughed. "No, no. Not a doctor like the ones here." he leaned back in his chair, crossing his legs. "But I've been called a doctor before."

I felt my body waking up from the numbness, crying out that I'm in some sort of danger, sitting with this extremely relaxed looking man and all alone, but my interest was piqued. I remember the smell of him. He was rich and herby, but floral. Once I smelled him, I found it harder to look away. I needed to find out what he could do.

"What kind of doctor are you?"

He had his legs crossed, foot bouncing on his knee, and he leaned forward and smiled. His teeth gleamed white except for the left canine that was plated in gold. He looked around to make sure we were alone and whispered, "The witchin' kind."

I'd lived in Naples my entire life and gone through a Wiccan phase in high school, so I'd heard of Witch Doctors before. They were always portrayed as purveyors of evil and darkness, a stark contrast to the man who sat before me with his yellow flip flop dangling off his raised foot.

"What is it you would want in return?" *I need to use caution here.*

"So you've heard of me then." His smile grew wider. "I want an even trade, that's all. Not asking too much, really." He produced a toothpick and placed it in his mouth, leaned back into the chair and folded his hands in his lap, looking up at the ceiling.

"What would you consider a fair trade for a life?" I asked.

"Not a life, a soul." he said. Chewing his wooden pick he lazily looked around everywhere but at me.

"Whose soul. Mine?"

He shrugged. "Seems fair, don't it? Your boy will live, and you will survive it too, don't worry."

"But...what happens— "

"Sorry to rush you," he snapped forward in his chair. His smile vanished and his smell filled my nostrils, making my eyes flutter, "I got other people I need to see. If you ain't interested, I best be moving on." He stood and turned to walk away, pulling a hat from beside him on the seat that I hadn't noticed and placing it on his head. A canary yellow fedora, of all ungodly things. *Maybe he is evil.*

"Wait!" I shouted just before he turned a corner. *If he's here, he must know something. He said it's a fair deal he wants, does that mean he's collecting a soul regardless? If he doesn't take my soul, will he take Everett's?* "What do I need to do?"

He turned around and his smile was back. "Come with me. No time to waste." he said and hustled down the hall, leaving me to catch up. He disappeared down the stairwell and by the time I caught him in the parking lot, I was out of breath and squinting. The sun blinded me as it met the horizon. *How long have I been here?*

"Get in. We need to make it there before the sun sets fully, otherwise things might not go so well."

He opened the door to an old tan Lincoln and reached over to unlock the passenger side. I looked over my shoulder at the plain grey building and he shouted out to me, "Your boy will be safe with the doc's in there."

I tore myself away from the hospital, pulled in by the scent of herbs spilling from the car. I had to leave. Had to leave so I could save him.

I slammed the car door as the engine roared to life. There was a beaded car seat cover across the entire front seat that clacked with every bump in the road. As we drew closer to the edge of town, I had to ask, "Where are we going and what happens if we don't get there before the sun sets?"

He sucked on his toothpick a couple of times, rolled down the window with an electric whir, and threw it out.

"I need the light to trade your souls. If we don't have a little bit of light," he shrugged, "won't work."

"And where are we going?"

He glanced over at me and shrugged, "My house, of course."

Of course, random mystery stranger. Of course.

We rolled off the road and into a driveway I would never have seen if we hadn't turned onto it. The dense foliage rolled by the window and we drove deeper up the drive. The canopy blocking most of the sun coming through and taking us into another world.

The house, or rather the shack, came into view and I don't exaggerate when I tell you dueling banjos wouldn't be out of place on its front step. Black and orange chickens roamed the yard and skittered out of the way as we parked, clucking with indignation.

"We need to be quick." the man said, and was out the door and into the house as fast as a python. I followed him in, the interior was tidy with dated furniture in a large open space. Not what I had expected from the rundown exterior. It was old, certainly, but it was clean and smelled like hibiscus. A pre-war era fan circulated the air with a low hum and the dusty beige curtains moved slightly with each pass.

He threw open a trunk and pulled out a mason jar, unscrewing the lid. He poured the black peppery substance down in a circle on an area rug that looked like it had seen plenty of use, then pointed to the middle. "Stand there," he said. No more smiling, no more beguiling. He was all business. "We're only getting one shot."

He hurried out into the yard as I stepped across the line of the stinky black powder. I thought about all the dead chickens and the blood spraying everywhere that you see in movies surrounding Hoodoo. With that thought, the extreme heat and humidity of the shack, and the stench of rotten eggs the powder gave off, I threw up a bit in my mouth.

He came back in and held a wooden staff that had a circle of dried reed bound to the top and a purple gemstone tangled in its center. He went to the curtain and slid the staff into a ring that jutted out at the base of the window. "Stay perfect and still. Right *there*." he said, fiddling with the staff until the purple caught the failing light. It flashed across my face and blinded me.

"Does that need to be in my eyes?"

"Course. They're the window." he said.

Of course. I forced my eyes open. *What good are they if I can't see Everett again?* I'd thought.

He started to chant, but I don't know what he said. He didn't speak Creole or French, like I expected, and it certainly wasn't English. I don't think it was a language that humankind used anymore. It was something that was long ago lost in the swamp and it rolled and slithered past his lips. The curtains billowed in and the shack filled with the scent of moss and still water and the screams of birds. He chanted louder to be heard over the din, and I stood as still as I could. I let that amethyst light blind me in the hopes that I hadn't gone insane, that I was doing something to save my son instead of waiting helplessly, reading about fucking alligators in a magazine.

He stopped chanting. "It's done." he said and shifted the light from my face. I blinked, but all I could see were purple spots everywhere and my eyes hurt. "Let's get you back to your boy now. He'll be wantin' to see you."

I nodded and stumbled my way to the door, *That's it? That was the big spell?* "Is that all?"

"Did you need something else? I offer many services, though you've given me your biggest bargaining chip already." He smiled and pointed at the stone that was glowing. Not from the sunlight, which was quickly fading, but from inside. Like something was trapped within. He plucked it from the string and put it in a worn leather pouch. The pouch glowed when he opened it, like there were plenty more souls inside. "I could take your eyes and give you the ability to see the future? Maybe you would like to give me your toes and I will make someone fall in love with you?"

A shiver rolled up my spine and I felt like the bargain might not have been as harmless as I'd thought.

"I don't need anything." I rubbed my temples, a dull pounding had come on from the stress and the witchy weirdness. "Take me back to Everett. Please."

He pointed to the door and flashed me his golden canine. "After you, Lydia."

I walked toward the door and rubbed my eyes as I crossed the porch. I opened them as the floor fell out from under my feet. I thought I had missed a stair, but instead of hitting the ground, I swirled through a purple cloud of smoke, falling endlessly as I let out a scream that ripped my throat to shreds.

I jerked awake in my purple chair at the hospital, the bloody tea towel still clutched in my fingers. I dropped it and looked around, rubbing my eyes. *What the hell just happened? Was that a dream?*

I heard the padding of soft soled shoes as the doctor who admitted Everett approached me. "Mrs. Cole?"

"Yes. Is Everett going to be okay?"

"He seems to be doing fine. We closed up the scratch with some butterfly stitches and you guys can head home now."

"We can?"

She looked at me, her eyebrows knitted together. "He had a mild laceration. It was on his neck, but it was nothing serious. Go home. You look like you need some rest. He's right there, room 418." She patted my arm as she bustled off to another crisis, and I felt like a rock had been lifted off my chest, allowing me to breathe.

I went to the room and Everett was sitting on the end of the bed, snacking on a jello cup. The colour had returned to his cheeks and he had a small bandage taped over the wound.

I moved to the bed, unable to comprehend this miracle. I pulled back the gauze to see the cut. A minor laceration with a few butterfly stitches.

"Mom, are you okay?" he asked.

I walked out of the room, building speed as I headed to the waiting room. I found the towel lying beside my chair and I turned it over in my hands to see only the faintest line of blood splashing one of the flower's petals. A cold wash and the towel would be restored.

Tears flowed down my hot cheeks. *It worked, it really worked; I saved him.*

"Mom?" Everett said, standing behind me. "Can we go home now?"

"Yes, dear. Let's go get tacos first though. I bet you're starving."

A quick stop at Taco Bell (not the quality we normally go for, but it was late), and we made it home a little before midnight. Bath time skipped, and exhaustion sinking in, Everett headed straight to bed with no complaints, closing his door behind him.

My adrenaline fired through me as I replayed the evening. My brain whirled through the details and events that transpired, wondering, *did it all really happen? Was it some sort of dream?* But I couldn't convince myself that the things I saw were apparitions. I knew it was real, I felt that gem burn into my eyes and saw the glow once the Witch Doctor was done.

I thought about calling John, but it was too late and there was nothing I could tell him at that point that wouldn't make me sound insane. I flicked on the television to see if I could find anything to watch and settled on an old sitcom I'd seen a hundred times. The live audience laughed and I could feel myself nodding off.

The clock in the hall chimed once and jolted me awake. I shut off the tv and headed to bed. *Half past twelve. Long past my bedtime.*

I made it to the top of the stairs and the hair on the back of my neck tingled, sending shivers across my skin. I whipped around, expecting to see the intruder had come back, but no one was there.

A breeze blew again and I heard the curtains rattle on the patio door. The door I thought I'd closed.

I headed back down the stairs and the curtains kept clacking as the breeze came through the open door. Little gusts of breath pushing them in.

Whoosh. Clack. Whoosh. Clack.

I went to close it, my skin crawling, and saw Everett's scooter sitting out on the patio. The scooter that almost ended his life.

I told him every damned day to put that thing away.

I grabbed the scooter, overcome with rage at the simplest and stupidest thing, and threw it towards the pool with all my might. The handlebars whacked my arm on the way by, making it go numb. It missed by a mile and I felt like an idiot for throwing it. I rubbed my arm and cursed, inspecting the soon-to-be bruise before I looked at the scooter again. That's when I saw it.

Across the pool and just outside the reach of the patio lights stood the black shape of a massive hound with its shoulders bunched up and ready to lunge. Its eyes glowed like hot coals, swirling with orange and yellows as it eyed me up.

I tried to run. I tried to pull my eyes away from the swirling madness I saw in that giant black beasts eyes, but I froze, and the hound launched itself at me.

I screamed, but it cut short as I felt it's teeth pierce the skin on my throat. Felt it's hot breath on my face for an instant before my blood was pouring down the front of my shirt and onto the grass.

I fell to the ground and the hound gave me a shake. I felt my neck cartilage crack. All the pain in my body, all the nerves misfiring and sending panic signals, stopped. I couldn't feel the patio beneath me, or the breeze on my exposed arms. I felt only cold as the hound trotted away, its work finished, and the light faded to black.

For the briefest of seconds, I laid there in darkness, unable to feel my body and thinking about Everett upstairs in his room, safe in bed.

In my last flicker of consciousness I thought to myself; *Fair trade.*

Dead in Apt. 3C

I used to have this neighbour who every evening, between the hours of seven and eight, would smoke pot on his balcony and cough deep, chesty coughs. It was usually at this time that he would also fire up his prehistoric microwave. I had always thought he inherited it from a long dead grandmother or something, but never got around to asking him. He would fire it up and the lights would flicker. The smell of cheap meat and cheese would fill the halls to cling to the moldy wallpaper and crusty carpet that lined them. It mixed with the smells of all the other meals being prepared in the poorly ventilated apartment and would linger for hours.

You would think that I'd find this annoying, but I didn't. I found it reassuring for some reason. It was like, if Johnny's getting high, then the world is a-okay. Everything is how it should be. Copacetic. Ya know?

It was the night Johnny didn't make his appearance on the balcony that shit got real.

I'd gotten home a bit early. My boss was feeling generous and closed the movie store down for his niece's bat mitzvah, and we all got to go home without pay. I was fine with it though. Really. I had never been keen on working, and the movie store was the longest I had ever lasted anywhere. My step-dad always said it was because my Mom babied me, but I think I was just wired different.

So I snagged the last copy of *Dawn of the Dead* from the shelf, palmed a package of peanut M&M's and said goodnight to Mr. Gold. I exited *Gold's Video Rentals and Games Emporium* and headed home to my bachelor pad.

I had no plans, except now to watch the newest zombie flick, so when I got home I called up my buddy Brad.

"I got the night off, you down for some Dawn of the Dead action?"

"Romero or that new shitty remake?"

"The new one. Wait, you've seen it?"

"Yeah, I downloaded it last week. The cinematography was trash, it looked like it was filmed on a potato."

"Maybe that's because you downloaded it, moron. For a college kid, you're not so bright. Come over and watch it with me."

He sighed and I knew I had him. "I'll come over after study group. See you then." he said, and clicked off.

Brad had gone to the University of Minnesota, making his parents proud, and I had decided that I wanted to take a year off. Just be out in the world for a little while and figure out some stuff. I figured I had time for college after. What's the rush?

Seven o'clock rolled around, and the lights started to flicker, which was weird because I hadn't heard Johnny coughing yet. I decided he must have changed up his routine and I went back to playing *Halo* while waiting for Brad to show up. That's when I heard a thump come from Johnny's place.

It was a small thump, followed up by a much larger thump on our shared wall. It rattled my CD racks and I thought for sure someone was going to Kool-aid man right through the bitch.

I paused my game, making sure to save, and went toward the wall. I pulled my hair back over my ear and leaned in to see if I could hear anything else.

Silence.

I stood there for longer than I would have normally. I heard something like a groan coming through the wall, but I wasn't sure. I couldn't hear shit over the Xbox's loud humming, so I shut it off and went back to the wall. I held my breath and pressed my ear against the wall.

The wall shook again, the impact landing squarely where my ear was. I'm not ashamed to admit that I screamed like a little girl and fell on my ass trying to put some distance between me and whatever was trying to come through the drywall.

I put my elbows on my knees, pressed my palms into my eyes and shouted, "Hey Johnny! Not fucking funny, man!" more pissed that I fell down than at the noise.

I turned the Xbox back on and was about to jump into another round when I thought, *shit, what if Johnny's hurt over there or something?* And I remembered seeing in health class that the best way to keep yourself from choking if you were alone was to throw yourself on a chair. *Is Johnny throwing himself around over there?*

I decided it was worth checking up on him, just in case he had choked on a bagel bite or something, and headed over to his door.

The hall smelled like it normally did, a blend of dry rot, mixed with mold, hot salami and skunk weed. Which I had thought was weird, since I hadn't heard him coughing like he normally did.

I knocked on the door and the lights faded, flickered and hummed back to life.

"Hey, Johnny, you in there?" I said, "Open up! It's me, Adrian!"

No reply. No thumping. No gurgles of a bong or swearing or AC/DC playing. *Oh my God, he's dead in there.* I'd thought.

"Alright, man, I'm coming in!" I said and tried the handle, which was unlocked but chained, so at least I could get a bit of a peek inside.

Johnny's kitchen was to the right of the door, where mine was to the left, so I was able to see in there. Apart from the stack of dishes and the overflowing trash can, there hadn't been much to see. That was until I spotted the urn.

On the counter, next to the first ever invented microwave, sat a metal urn. It was a flat black and had an upside down cross on it. I remembered Johnny had gone to a funeral for one of his pals yesterday. He'd said his buddy went crazy and started to try and bite people in a Wal-Mart before he was shot by the responding police.

"Johnny!" I yelled through the door, "Open up!"

I heard a shuffle, followed by running feet and the door slammed so hard in my face I thought it was going to come off the hinges.

"Holy fuck, dude! Chill!" I said, but he pounded the door again, the frame jumped and dust particles filled the air, making that dry rot smell even worse. I covered my face with my shirt. It didn't smell much better, but I figured it wouldn't have asbestos in it.

"AAADDAANNN..." Johnny groaned and then threw himself at the door again, making the wood creak and jump.

"My name's Adrian, you dick. We've played *Halo* together like ten times, how do you not remember that?"

"AAAADDDAAADDDAANN..." he said again, and I figured he must have lost it.

His friend. Shit, what if he has whatever his friend had? I thought.

He slammed into the door again and one of the hinges gave way, tilting the door to the side, which made him go even more berserk.

"AAADAAN, AADAA!" He moaned at me and bashed the door with his fists before backing up to take another run at it.

"Fuck this." I said, and ran back to my apartment.

I slammed the door, bolted it, chained it and then shoved my kitchen chair under the knob just to make sure before I grabbed the phone to call the police. "Sorry, Johnny," I said, punching in 911, "Hope they don't shoot you too."

Another crash, the door came free, and Johnny groaned some more. The operator answered with a chipper, can-do attitude. I felt a bit like hanging up and trying again. My door shook with the impact of Johnny throwing himself at it to get to me, and I decided I could deal with it.

"Hey there, my neighbour is kinda going nuts and trying to break into my apartment."

"Okay then. Do they have any weapons?" she said.

The door banged and the chair shook under the knob. "No, no weapons that I know of. He's using his body like some sort of battering ram though."

"I'm sorry, a battering ram?"

"Yeah, like what they used to invade castles. You know, the big wooden things and they would hit the door with it?"

"So he has no weapons?"

The door shook again and I heard a panel crack. "No. No weapons. Can you send someone over here? My door is really old, and I don't think it can take much more punishment."

"Okay, sir. Where are you located?"

"I'm in those shitty grey apartments out on Ashwood Lane. Apartment 3C."

"Alright, I know where you mean. I have a unit on their way to check things out for you.

Now, I'm going to stay on the line with you until they arrive, alright sweetie? Do you have anything nearby that you can defend yourself with?"

Sweetie? Ugh "I have some plates, and a couch, and a—"

"Do you have anything like a bat, or maybe a big knife or something along those lines?"

The hinges creaked and the wood panel on the door exploded inward to reveal Johnny's face on the other side of the door. I felt like he missed an opportunity at that point, it's not every day that someone named Johnny punches a hole in a door in a homicidal episode. Instead of saying, 'here's Johnny!' like he obviously should have, he said, "AAADDDAAANN!"

"Hey, Johnny." I said to the blue and purple face that was trying to wedge through the opening. "Hey, lady, can you hold on for just a minute? I need to push my couch up against the door."

I put the phone down on the counter. The operator lady said something, but I didn't hear it, and pushed the couch up against the door. It was my parents' old hide-a-bed couch, so it took some doing. I thought Johnny would probably make it through the door soon. I heard Mr. Yakobo shout about the noise in the hall, then he promptly slammed his door again and Johnny went after him.

I picked up the phone off the counter then, "Hey, I'm back. He just went after Mr. Yakobo."

"They're on the way. I have sent another car out to you as well. Do you have a bat?" she said, her voice not as nice as it had been at the beginning of our talk.

"Right, a bat. I do have a bat." I told her and went to my bedroom.

I heard Mr. Yakobo's door splinter into kindling and he screamed out something in swahili. There was a bunch of shouting then, and I don't know if it was Johnny or Mr. Yakobo. As quick as it started, it stopped, and the halls were silent again.

"I think Johnny got Mr. Yakobo." I said.

"Did you find your bat?" the lady asked, her voice seemed tense.

"Yes. I have it now. It's an aluminum tee ball bat, do you think that will work?"

"It's better than nothing." she said. Her voice was muffled, and I got the feeling she had put her head down on her desk.

"Hello? Adrian?" I heard someone call through the door.

"Brad!" I had forgotten that he was coming over to watch *Dawn of the Dead*. How ironic.

"What the fuck is going on out here? There's a door hanging off here and that ones smashed in...and your door has a fucking hole in it. What're you doing in there, is that your couch?"

"Brad, listen; Johnny's lost it, and he's attacked Mr. Yakobo."

"He wha–"

"Just shut up for a second! I'm going to move the couch and you can come in here until the cops come."

I set the phone back on the counter and pulled the couch down with a thud. The springs reverberated, humming inside the folded up bed. I moved the kitchen chair and unlocked the door, opening it just in time to see Brad get tackled by Johnny, sending him sprawling down the hall like a crash test dummy. Mr. Yakobo was right behind him. He came after me, but he lost some of his speed trying to turn a ninety degree corner at a full run. His ankle buckled and made a horrible popping noise as he fell in front of me. I saw my chance and I took it. I swung my mini-bat as hard as I could onto his shiny bald head.

I weighed about a hundred and ten pounds, and had never swung a bat before in my life. This was actually the last tenant's bat, or his kid's I guess, so I didn't do much damage. The bat glanced off his skull and Mr. Yakobo stood up, his ankle jutting off to the side, and he came for me again. His ankle crunched every time he stepped down on it, and I thought I was gonna hurl.

Johnny appeared in the doorframe, and I knew Brad was toast. And after all that studying to get into U of M. God damned shame really. At least I got a bit of freedom before I died.

Mr. Yakobo and Johnny kept coming forward, walking much more slowly now, like they knew I was trapped on the third floor with no escape and a stupid mini bat. I backed down the hall and hoped like hell that the cops would show up now. I didn't care much if they shot Johnny in the head now. In fact, it was all I thought about as they closed in on me.

I tried to make a dash for the bedroom door, hoping to live a smidge longer, but as soon as I turned to run, they pounced.

Johnny landed on top of me and my ribs cracked. They popped like dried twigs and I couldn't breathe. Stars filled my eyes and I tried to scream. *How the hell did it get to this?* I remember thinking as Mr. Yakobo chomped down on my achilles tendon. I felt the sinew snap and he pulled at it with his teeth, tugging the cord until it broke off at my knee and slithered out my leg.

I wished for death then. I had never really thought about it before, but it seemed better than the pain I was in.

Johnny kept on top of me, content to keep crushing all the air out of my body, then Brad showed up. He shoved his way past

Mr. Yakobo and Johnny and made for the last bit of me that wasn't already taken. His skin was the same blueish purple as Johnny's, and Mr. Yakobo's, and he didn't hesitate to grant me my last wish.

He dropped to his knees and sunk his teeth into my neck. All I could think about as he tore out my jugular was that his parents had put out a lot of money for braces on his teeth. All so he could chew me to death.

I heard a command shouted from the doorway (the cops showing up far too late) and the bastards that were chewing on me all turned toward the sound in unison. Brad dropped my head to the floor and my blood shot out at the wall, coating the white paint. It shot out in spurts, matching the rhythm of my heart, the spurts slowing, slowing, slowing, until finally, my vision failed and the blood stopped.

Ruby Tuesday

———

It was 2:11 a.m. when I woke up. The harsh red glare of the alarm clock was the only light in the pitch dark room.

I'd slept for two hours and woken with that morning's argument ringing in my ears. Layla had left for Michigan. She had to, her new position at the University started next week, and she needed to get settled in at her folks place.

We'd talked about it, talked for what felt like an eternity, and I had caved in the end. As much as I wanted my freedom, far away from Ann Arbor and my parents, I wanted Layla more.

She had worked towards this for so long, and now she could finally move back and teach at U of M. Not a shitty assistant position, but as a full time Biochemistry professor. It was the big leagues, and I wanted to go. To be there for her.

Like I usually did, I chickened out.

I couldn't go back. I didn't want to deal with my parents. I didn't want to have them poking into our lives and asking questions about our relationship like they gave a shit. All the while they'd be shifting uncomfortably in their seats when they thought about us both having vaginas.

Looking at it now, I don't know if they were bigots in their hearts, but I *do* think that they never thought about our 'kind' until I came out. It was new and scary, and they didn't want to deal.

Fair enough, neither did I, and that's why I stayed behind in Wisconsin.

Layla had left, sure I just needed some time, and I had spent the rest of the day hating myself. Now it was 2:11 am and my head wanted to split in half.

I got up and threw on a sweatshirt and cap. I slipped on my slippers and jumped in my car. The engine squealed to life, ticking off time as I headed down the road.

I pulled into the Gas-N-Gulp, the only place open at this hour, and headed inside. The cold fluorescent lights pierced into my brain, and I wondered how the clerk managed to not kill himself every night.

"You got any Tylenol?" I asked him.

"Sure, right back here." he said, spinning around and grabbing a bottle from the shelf. "You want regular or extra strength?"

I looked him in the eye and he grinned.

"Alright, extra strength then." He scanned the miniscule bottle with a deafening beep and put it in a bag. "Anything else?"

I shook my head and handed him a ten. He took it and the register opened in union to the sound of my car squealing to life outside.

I whipped around and saw the headlights flickering as the bucket of bolts spun around and the thief floored it.

"Isn't that your car?" the clerk said.

I sighed and grabbed the bag, looking at his name tag. "Yes, Alex. That was my car. And no, I don't have theft insurance. Who would ever want to steal that piece of shit?" as if to punctuate my point, the car backfired as it roared away and out of sight.

"Sorry. Rough night." he said.

"Yeah." I walked toward the door and he called after me.

"Do you need a cab or something? What about your change?"

I didn't have the will to converse any longer, so I waved and started to walk down the road, letting the *bee-bong* of the door answer for me. It was only two miles. *Maybe a walk will help clear my head.* I'd thought, *alright universe. I'm walkin'. I wish I hadn't worn my fuckin' slippers.*

The wind blew and I could smell leaves. It smelled like fall was coming. Like the air was crisper. Cleaner. Like the wind was ready to start knocking leaves off trees, even though it was only September.

The road back to my house was quiet, except for the wind. The street lamps in this neighborhood were a dull orange and I wondered if the bulbs had ever been changed in them. *How long do lightbulbs like that last anyway?* I sighed and stopped to open the pills. *I wish Layla were here. She'd know. She knows everything.*

I got through the three layers of packaging and childproofing, and when I opened the bottle, it lept from my hands, spilling ten little white pills on the ground.

"God dammit! Why?" I shouted and shook my fists at the inky sky.

I bent down and picked up two pills and blew on them. *Screw the rest of it*, I'd thought, popping the pills down the hatch, swallowing them dry. One of them slid down rough and I had a moment of panic thinking I would choke to death on the side of a road in the middle of the night. Boy was *I* wrong.

Once I'd finished my coughing fit, I looked up and saw someone standing a block ahead. They looked tall, six feet or maybe more, and weighed about a buck ten soaking wet. They just stood there, the light shining on their strange wide brimmed hat and casting a shadow over their face.

I blinked and they were gone.

"What the–" I rubbed my eyes, one at a time so I wouldn't look away from the spot, but they didn't reappear. "That was fuckin' odd." I said, "And now I'm talking to myself."

I started to shuffle toward the spot, keeping my eyes roving around to see if they would reappear. The wind blew and it felt like breath on my neck. I turned, but no one was there.

The hair on my neck stood on end as I drew close to the street light. I stopped under its weak amber glow and it flickered, making my stomach drop. I spun around. The feeling of being watched from the darkness made me want to bolt, and I nearly fainted when I saw the person standing under the light I was just at.

"What the shit." I said to myself.

The figure didn't move, it just stood there under the light with its hat shadowing its face. I stared it down, thinking if I didn't move it would go away. Like it was a t-rex or something.

I could feel its eyes on me. Prying into me like they could see through my clothes, through my skin and down to my bones. It looked at me like it wanted to taste my bones, like it wanted to suck the marrow from my femur beside a fire in a cave.

*What the fuck is that thing...it's not human...*I'd thought.

Its long praying mantis like leg jutted toward me and it took a step forward. I nearly jumped out of my skin and took a step back, remembering what I'd learned about running from a dog. You never want to run from a dog. That's when they get you.

It took another step, its legs moving in impossibly long strides as its arms dangled by its sides. Its whole body was out from under that orange light now, and with only the moonlight to see it by, it looked even more terrifying. Just a long and awkward black shape taking lurching steps toward me as I tried to back away.

It was gaining on me, its legs easily twice the length of mine. I took another step, and without having looked away from the thing rapidly gaining on me, I stepped right off the curb.

My slippers went flying and I screamed, landing flat on my back, sending my diaphragm into spasms and the air from my lungs.

If I had any air then, I would have used it to keep screaming. The thing took three steps in rapid succession and was nearly on me as I scrambled to my feet. I glanced back at it and in the dim starlight, I caught a glimpse of its face. I ran harder.

Its skin was like marble, pale and creamy white with blue veins snaking through it. It was gaunt, like it hadn't eaten in a century, and the tightness of the skin on its skull made its teeth stick from beneath its lips. Its tongue lolled to the side in anticipation of the marrow it would get from my pretty little bones. Its teeth were bared, but they weren't what I expected. I thought they would be sharp, like a wolf or some sort of predator, but they were distinctly human in every way but size.

They stuck out from its mouth, three sizes too big, straight and perfect, like they were designed to crush you to powder. The block-like teeth shone pearlescent in the moonlight, and I wondered how he kept them so clean, given how dirty the rest of his black suit was.

I pumped my arms harder, and my bare feet went numb from the cold. Not numb enough to ignore the stray rocks and other various hard and sharp objects that crashed through the skin of my soles, sending bullets of pain up my spine.

My stamina was failing and I started to slow, regretting not joining Layla on her morning runs and opting to sneak cigarettes instead. I threw a glance over my shoulder, and the thing was gone.

I stopped dead in my tracks, sure I was walking into some sort of ambush, and did a three sixty. I slowly scanned the surrounding shrubbery and fences, trying to find where this nightmare had disappeared to.

All I could hear was my heart pounding in my head and the ragged pull of my lungs as I tried to suck in more oxygen. My body shook and my head felt like it was being jackhammered, but I couldn't see it.

Wait...

In the hedge, thirty feet away and to my left, there was a gap in the branches. I stared into it, thinking I could see something shift in the darkness. It was black on black, so I couldn't be sure.

I took a step closer, trying to see, willing my breath to slow to normal. I took another step, and the black hole slowly changed to a gaunt face. The pale skin creaked like worn leather as the things jaw distended and the teeth were suddenly proportionate to its mouth as it grew large enough to throw a football in.

"No!" I screamed at it, but its eyes never left me. Its mouth kept growing, and it burst from the hedge and ran towards me on stilt thin legs.

I barely had time to turn, but I had time to think as the adrenaline coursed through my body and all my synapsis fired at once.

I felt my ankle twist and the ligament pop. I thought about how Layla always put too much sugar in her coffee.

I lost my balance and started to fall. I remembered that Christmas when Layla learned how to knit and made me a toque that was big enough we could both wear it at the same time.

I hit the ground and felt the impact shudder up through my palms and remembered the first time we talked. How she had bit her lip and I thought it was cute, only to find out later it was something she only did when she was exceptionally nervous.

I couldn't catch myself and my face hit the asphalt, busting my lip and bloodying my nose as my senses came back to me just in time to feel the monster's mouth close around my leg.

I screamed.

A light popped on in the house closest to me and a dog inside barked.

It chomped down at my knee, and the wet feeling of its throat on my skin was replaced by the blazing pain where my leg had been shorn off by its massive teeth.

I thought there was still hope, so I kept screaming, "Help me! Somebody help!" as I heard it gulping and gnashing, my bones grinding and crunching in its cave of a mouth.

I tried to crawl away, but it was still hungry and was crawling after me on its hands and knees as it finished swallowing my leg. Its movements on the ground looked more smooth, more natural. Like it was built to run on four legs.

I kicked at it, but its mouth just opened and clamped down on my other leg, taking it too. I tried to pull myself further away as it ground my tibia down like kibble. The adrenaline that would have helped me run was helping the blood pump out of my exposed arteries as fast as possible.

I felt a wave of dizziness and nausea swarm over me as I saw it still crawling after me, its stomach distended from snacking on my legs. The buttons on its suit jacket strained to hold in its sudden bulk.

My palm slipped and I fell backward as it grabbed my hips and pulled me towards its mouth. My strength was gone, and I couldn't even flinch as it chomped down on my thigh. My body had numbed, but I could smell its rancid breath as it gobbled on me.

My brain was done, it had seen enough, and I was losing consciousness as a shot rang out. A bullet winged the thing that was eating me.

It dropped me to the asphalt and sprinted off into the darkness on all fours, elbows and knees jutting out like an arachnid.

"Jesus Christ, what the hell's he done to you, darlin'." said a voice beside me.

"Layla..." I whispered, and the world fell to black as the stranger's dog sniffed my ear.

Moth at the Window

———

My phone buzzed, another message from the ex-lover boy at the library. I pushed the volume button, not bothering to flip open and read the message. I already knew what it'd say. *Tiff, you're the one, I need you to come back to me.* There's only so many ways I could say, 'and I need another hole in my head.'

The air was chilly. I cursed my grandparents for not having proper heating, only an old wood furnace in the basement. I shuffled downstairs, my faithful terrier Larry at my ankle as always. I headed to the main floor and let him out to do his thing. A fog was rolling into town with the cool evening air. Nothing was visible past my fence line, but the flickering amber streetlamp was trying to turn on. Most people hate the fog, but I kind of loved it. It's so mysterious and kind of creepy. Maybe that's why I fell for my new guy, Mitch; a love of the mysterious.

I don't know what it was about him, but he made my knees weak. Literally. When he kissed me, he had to help prop me up so I wouldn't fall to the floor. Seeing him made my heart beat faster, and my stomach drop. Things had been on the fritz with Tony for a while, and meeting Mitch...well, it must have been a sign. I broke it off with Tony the next day, or it might have been the next week...either way. We'd been through for a couple weeks, and I was with Mitch.

Larry came bounding to me through the fog, racing inside like something was chasing him. I turned and headed into the basement. The fire had burned down to embers, but some kindling fired it up. Another log would last until my date with Mitch. I had to hurry up if I wanted to be ready for him. My sister was expecting me to have a box of Grann's wedding photos for her. She was coming by, and I wanted her gone long before Mitch came over, but I still hadn't found them up in the attic.

My grandparents died last year in a horrible car accident. I'd been going through the piles of old stuff (mostly junk) in the attic and donating it or re-homing it with family. They left the house to me, but the only reason I got the place was because I'm a fuck up. My other sisters are married and have kids, but not the loser Tiff. She can't keep a man, can't keep a job, can't keep the fridge stocked. Basically, as far as my grandparents were ever concerned, I just couldn't keep up.

I pulled the door down from the ceiling with a creak. A fresh powdering of dust rained down along with cobwebs and God knows what else. I looked up the ladder at the opening to the attic. The black hole stared back. It looked like it could hide any number of spiders, ghosts or long lost grandkids my family never told me about. I shivered. It's stupid. To look into something like an attic and feel like death is staring back at you. Stupid or not, I hoisted Larry up there first to give a good sniff around before crawling up after him.

I nearly fell scrambling for the string to turn the light on. The bulb swung on its wire, throwing shadows in crazy directions.

The dancing light did little to stop the pounding in my heart or the power of my imagination. Larry looked up at me, eyebrows crinkled and head cocked. I imagined him thinking, *she's doing that thing again.*

I took a deep breath, "Yeah, I know. It's just an attic. Nothing scary up here." the shadows stilled and I turned on the next light. The warm orange glow made it less ominous, and I bent down to give my good boy a scratch, "Thanks for checking it out, Larry. I can always count on you."

I looked at the boxes and then my watch. I needed to be ready in another hour, and there were boxes up to the rafters. "Needle in a haystack." I said, and shook my head. "Music?" I asked Larry. He sneezed and I took that as a yes, moving to the old record player and flipping the switch. A little red light blinked on and I slid a record out of its sleeve, laying it down on the velvet pad. I pushed a button and the arm swung, clicking into place as the record started its rotations. The needle fell into the track and the cobwebs no longer mattered as the first notes rang out. My task felt a bit more possible after that.

Mon Diue blared through the grainy old speakers and I moved the boxes around, throwing even more dust in the air. *I hope there's no crazy killer spores up here,* I'd thought. Larry sneezed his agreement, reading my mind like always. Edith Piaf finished and the horn opening blared for *La vie en Rose.* The French trilled and touched my soul. It was like some distant ancestor reaching out to me through time and space. I pulled a box down and, low and behold, the grand prize!

I set the box down and the needle jumped, setting Edith into a fit of *la vie-la vie-la vie*. I stood to fix the record and hit the string light with my head, not paying attention to where I was going. The bulb smashed and a pop of electricity made me shriek. Larry whimpered and I pulled the switch before electrocuting myself on the exposed filaments. Edith kept jumping as I pulled glass out of my hair and made my way over to shut her up. A broken record is the worst noise in the world, other than maybe nails on a chalkboard. After the light exploded in my face, my nerves were shot. I pulled the needle off and hoped the record was repairable. It was my favourite, and always made me remember the good times when me and gran-papa would slow dance in the kitchen. His smoky smell hung heavy in my nose and his stubble scratched my cheek as we swayed.

The attic was heavy with silence and memories. Larry sat next to me, looking up with his big eyes and drooping ears. I picked him up and said, "It's okay, little man. Mommy was just a bit startled." I looked at the floor and all the glass littering it and gave him a kiss on the head, thankful he didn't step on any of the razorblade fragments.

In the silence, with my face pressed on Larry's soft little head, I heard a thump behind me. If I hadn't had my scared little dog with me, I might have screamed again, but he kept me grounded. Until I heard it again.

THUMP thump thump.

A stack of boxes laid between me and the noise, and I had visions of Michael Myers crouched with his kitchen knife.

"You're being stupid." I said and forced myself to creep toward the boxes.

THUMP thump thump.

I stopped in my tracks, all the hairs on my neck standing up. I felt Larry shiver and he let out a squeaky growl.

"It's nothing, Larry. It's okay." I said, and picked up an old lamp with my free hand while cradling him in the other.

I jumped around the edge of the boxes and screamed. There was no one there but the dust bunnies. I lowered the lamp as the sound went again. A moth the size of a mini jumbo jet was throwing itself at the small window in a vain attempt at escape.

"Not quite *Papillion*, are you little fella?" I said, and laughed at my joke. I put the lamp down, and my hand shook as I reached out to open the window. The moth fluttered off into the night, moving like a drunk toward the amber light of the streetlamp outside.

The fog was as dense as ever, but there was a stooped figure under the lamp. They peered up at me with shadows hiding their face. Even in the dark, I felt a shiver of recognition. "Grann?" I whispered as a second figure joined her.

Glass crunched behind me, and it felt like my heart stopped and time ceased. The empty light socket swayed and I called out, "Hello?"

Larry started to shiver again. I held my breath and looked around the attic without blinking when the sound came from behind me.

THUMP thump thump.

I didn't want to look away from the half dark attic, but the sound took me by surprise. I twisted around to see the moth back at the window. It thumped the pane of glass from the outside then flew toward the light where the stooped figure stood with the other. *Is that you, Grann?* Between the fog and the dark, it was impossible to tell. Whoever it was, it was time to get out of that spooky ass attic and investigate.

I picked up the lamp. "If there's anyone there, I'm leaving, and I've got a weapon!"

I crept to the ladder, glass crunching under slippered feet. My head moved around like an automatic sprinkler, scanning for whatever had made the noise. I turned and set the lamp down then crawled down as fast as I could, almost dropping poor Larry in the process. I slammed the trap door shut and ran to the door, snatching my cell from its charger on the way.

I turned around when the cold night air hit my face, but there was no pursuer. I stood there, breathing heavy, when the sound came from above me.

THUMP thump thump.

I looked up and saw the moth smashing itself against the window. I had no idea why it wanted back in so badly. The thought of throwing a match and committing insurance fraud crossed my mind.

The dark figure stood under the lamp, alone now, and despite the shadows, I felt them staring at me... like they knew me. The phone's light was near blinding as I flipped it open and dialed 9-1-1. The speaker blared as the pre-recorded voice told me the 'caller was unavailable' as I got close enough to see the figure.

"You don't need to do that anymore." she said, and my breath caught.

"Grann?" I said and dropped the phone to my side. "But...you're dead."

"Quite right, child." she nodded in that matter-of-fact way she did. "Dead as a doornail."

The damp foggy air stuck to me and a chill seeped down into my marrow. "Then how are you here?"

"I came to get you." She pointed to the house and I looked back, following her twisted arthritic finger.

Everything seemed like it always had. Dark green shutters, and a picket fence. Bone white siding that was due for a paint job in a couple years. But up in the attic, through that little window, an orange light shone into the night. The moth was thumping against the glass and behind it was a silhouette. I couldn't make out the face with the back lighting.

"Jesus fucking Christ! There's someone up there!" I shouted and pointed at the window.

"Yes, dear. There are two somebody's."

"Two? How do you know that? Wait–" I said, looking at my pointing hand, and feeling my phone in the other. "Where's Larry?" I spun around, but he wasn't anywhere nearby.

"Don't worry." Grann said, "He's up there. Hiding and safe. Neighbours will find him in the morning...and you."

"Me?"

She nodded and pointed up at the window. The face came closer. Hair in a bun on their head, caramel complexion with drop dead gorgeous brown eyes and full lips.

"Son of a bitch." I put a hand to my mouth. "That's me!"

"You don't have to watch what happens next. It's not pleasant." she said, and my eyes became glued to that tiny square at the top of the house.

My attic self straightened and a shadow cut across the light. I wanted to scream, to tell myself to look out, but it was too late. A hand drew across my throat, cutting a glistening crimson smile on my attic self's skin. I put my hand to my throat as I watched a pale face slide around my attic self's shoulder, chomping down on me and dragging me from view. My fingers came away wet and I looked away from the window in the attic to see a trail of blood leading to where I stood.

"What was that?" I whispered as a tear slid down my cheek, icy cold on my skin.

"Don't matter much." Grann said. "It's time to go now." I looked at her and saw the side of her face that was in the shadows. Her skull was sunken and an eye was missing with bits of raw flesh hanging from her cheekbone.

"Grann, your face!"

She shrugged. "Don't worry dear, I can't feel it. Just like you can't feel that." she pointed at my neck. "We live in the afterlife how we died in this one. Until we're through the black, that is." She turned and shuffled toward the street lamp, placing her hand on the steel pole. "Come now. It's past time we went." she said, holding out her other hand to me.

I walked toward her, my mind numb and my feet reluctant. I looked at my phone one last time and saw a message from Mitch.

Can I come in?

And my reply.

Yes.

As You Wish...

———

It'll stop. It has to stop. That's what I kept telling myself anyway. How could I know it would never stop? That the rage inside me would be with me forever. Even now, it's with me, but it's more of a dull ache than the searing rage that consumed my flesh.

I'd started the day like I did any other. I opened my eyes, looked at my phone. Got out of bed and brushed my teeth. I went to work, grabbing a nonfat caramel macchiato and a sous vide egg from Buckstar's on the way. Just like any other day.

It was raining, but that was typical. I hadn't been able to recall the last day there wasn't rain. I made it to the office nearly drip free and went to my cubicle, plugged in my headset at 9:01 and was off to the races. I pestered old people and stay-at-home Mom's. I called them, asking if they knew about a surefire way to lose that pesky belly fat, or if they'd heard of the newest scientifically proven way to get rid of dandelions.

My job sucked, but I needed the money. There wasn't much else for a guy like me. Nevermind my advanced degree in aerospace engineering. So I sold shitty products to gullible people and made minimum wage plus five percent commission. I scraped by, barely. Sometimes I even had enough money to send home to my folks.

3:30pm that day, my boss's assistant came over and asked me to come with him to see the big cheese. I gladly followed, enjoying the view of his broad shoulders and tight ass, never suspecting what was coming.

"You're firing me? What the fuck, Pete?"

"Look, Amir, it's not my call–"

"Bullshit it's, 'not your call', you run the fucking company!"

"I run this office, and I listen to corporate. They tell me you were the name they pulled out of a hat. I'm sorry."

He *had* looked genuinely sorry, but that didn't stop me from knocking over his stupid R2D2 pen holder and letting it smash on the floor. I couldn't believe they were firing me. I knew why they chose me, but what could I do about it? As much as I wanted to 'fight the man', I had no proof that it was because of my accent or because my visa was in an alphabet they didn't understand.

I collected my things and headed out, punching the button for the main floor hard enough that the woman in the elevator with me got out before the doors could shut. *Fine. Fuck you, lady.* I'd thought.

I got out under the canopy at the entrance, my sad cardboard box of belongings in hand, before I realized I'd forgotten my umbrella. The rain was coming down like it always did in Seattle, but I decided to say 'fuck it' to going back for it and just got wet instead.

Looking back now, I should've gone back for the umbrella. It would've been the rational thing to do, but I was furious. Rage had become my default. I'd lived in Seattle with no problems for years. I was on the verge of becoming a citizen, and in the blink of an eye, and because of the actions of someone who looked like me, I had everything taken away.

So, *fuck the umbrella*, had been my thought, and I tucked the picture of my parents and my little sister Mina in my coat and left.

The bus came and I got on it, my cardboard box soggy and my possessions ruined. All but the picture. I sat at the back of the bus, not wanting to deal with the people muttering about the bearded man with dark eyes, and flung the box of shit on the floor. I had an hour bus ride to get back to Shoreline.

No one sat near me on the way back, and I watched the buildings shorten and the boutique stores and coffee shops turn into quick-n-loans and pawn shops. The bus had nearly emptied as my neighborhood drew near, and a man came and sat beside me.

What the fuck is up with this guy? I'd thought. *No one will come near me, but this guy basically sits on my lap?*

The man's round face was dripping, and from the smell of him, I could tell it wasn't from the rain. He clutched onto a leather briefcase and kept muttering to himself, "No, no. I can't let you go. I can't let you hurt anyone else."

"Hey, buddy, you alright?" I asked.

"No!" he shut his eyes tight and clenched his teeth together, letting out a groan of pain as his face reddened.

"Hey, bus driver? I think we need to stop." I shouted to the front. The man's eyes snapped open and he grabbed me by the collar of my coat, shaking me like I was a small child, not the six foot tall buck ninety I was.

"We don't need his help!" He pleaded, spit flying off his lips and speckling my face. His eyes were glowing embers and his skin was smoldering, the sweat wicking away with the extreme heat coming off him. His voice changed, dropping an octave as he said, " You are weak, we need *him*!"

"What the fu–" I managed to say before the driver slammed the brakes and pulled the bus to the side of the road. Then the man did something really peculiar.

He kissed me.

His face was about a thousand degrees, and I smelled my beard hair burn, singed by his touch.

Kiss might have been a bit of an oversell, because what he was doing was more like aggressive and unnecessary CPR. His skin cooled and fire snaked down my throat, burning and tearing its way down into my belly. I wanted to scream, to let the world know I was not okay with this man blowing fire worms into my mouth, but all I could do was gurgle and try to cough the thing out.

The bus hit the curb in the driver's haste to get to whatever mess was happening on his rig, and it threw me and the man from our seats. I fell to the floor while the short accountant looking man ninja rolled and burst through the rear doors of the bus with the grace of a rhinoceros. The cold air rushed in and the rain sprayed into the cabin as I watched the man make a b-line into the park.

He made it about twenty yards before he burst into a ball of flame and fell. He burned on the ground outside, the rain unable to extinguish him, and I coughed at the smell of burning synthetic clothing, hair and flesh. The burns to my esophagus didn't help either.

The driver came back to check on me and said, "Jesus Mother Fuckin' Christ. That boy's on fire!"

"Y–" I managed before I coughed and decided to just nod my head in agreement.

"Let me help you out." The driver bent down and helped me get up and into a seat. "You alright?" he asked.

I rubbed my throat, the burning was going away. *That's weird.* I'd thought, but decided not to question it. "Yes, I think I am."

"You need me to call a doctor or something?"

"No, no. I think I'm good." I pointed to his crumpled door. "I hope they're not going to ding you for that."

"Shit. Me too." he shook his head. "I don't think I'm supposed to move the bus like this. You got far to go?"

"No, this is my stop actually."

"Thank God for small miracles, huh?"

I nodded and grabbed my soggy box while the driver radioed in that he needed a tow and that someone should call the fire department... and the coroner. I slipped away, not wanting the attention of xenophobic cops, and headed home.

The rain was still pelting down. When I got to my apartment, I threw the box directly into the dumpster, scaring an alleycat from its cover, and headed upstairs.

I was soaked through to my underwear when I started the climb. My roommates wouldn't be home yet, so I'd been looking forward to some time to myself before I had to tell them my portion of the rent might be late. Again.

I climbed the stairs slowly, my throat felt back to normal and I remember thinking, *Whatever that guy did to me, it didn't seem to stick.*

By the time I rounded the corner on the fourth floor landing, my clothes were dry and I was feeling a bit warm. "That's weird." I said to myself. *That guy had burst into flames, maybe I shouldn't have left so quickly.* I started to feel woozy then, but I managed to get the key into the lock despite there being three of them swimming in front of me.

I stumbled over to my room (mine and Maheer's) and I threw open the window, stripped down to my skivvies and collapsed onto my cot. I let the world sink into darkness as the rain drummed down on the roof and misty breezes blew across my hot skin.

<Wake up, Amir>, a deep, gravelly voice called to me in the darkness of my unconscious. <Wake up and serve. >

My eyes fluttered open and Maheer was standing over me with his arms crossed. "Have a good rest?" he said.

"Not really. It's hot in here, why'd you shut the window?"

"Because I don't want to start growing mold, that's why. The rain was pouring in all over the place, but you're not wet. What's going on?"

I sat up and held my head in my hands, "I don't know."

"Figure it out, and clean this up." He threw the towel he was holding at me and hit me in the face. I grabbed the towel, scowling at Maheer. I hated how he treated me like I was second class.

<Do not accept this affront. Kill him.> The voice from my dreams said.

"What? No, I'm not–" I said but my back stiffened and my legs brought me to my feet. "What the hell?" I shouted, but the world was swirling in front of me, mixing in with reds and oranges like looking through a disturbing kaleidoscope. Maheer's back was to me, walking from the room like he was in slow motion. My arms leapt in front of me and I wrapped the towel around his neck.

What's happening? Stop that! I shouted inside my head, my lips no longer in my command.

< You do not accost a djinn and live. > the voice said.

I wanted to ask what the hell a djinn was, how he had gotten inside my head, why he had chosen me, but all I could do was stand by in horror as my body turned away, hauling Maheer onto my back. I could feel him struggling against the tug of the towel wrapped around his neck, but he was no match for me even before I had a djinn powering my muscles. He only struggled for a moment as my body jerked him upward, pulling hard. The reverberation of his neck breaking rumbled up my arms and across my back, making my stomach flip-flop.

The djinn dropped Maheer and he landed with a thud. I didn't want to turn, but it made me look at him. His face was pale, eyes full of shock, and mouth open. His neck was bruised and crooked to the side at a nasty angle. My body wanted to throw up, *I* wanted to throw up, but the djinn didn't allow it.

It stepped over Maheer and dressed my body. My hands moved without my consent to button my shirt as I asked, *What are you gonna do to me?*

< You will serve as my vessel until you are unable, then I will find another to bear my flame. >

Bear your flame?

< Silence! >

You can't stop me from talking, it's my head!

< Then I will break you. Your rage brought me to you, I could feel that fire inside you and it allowed me to enter. Like kindling for

my essence. All it needed was my spark. > images of my office and of Peter, our argument, flashed in my mind. <*I think we will start there. You have a lot of rage for this man. I will use it to grow stronger. I will grant your wish.* >

No, I'm not mad at Peter, not really. He just-

<*You can not lie to me, Amir. I am inside of you. I know your heart.* >

My heart?

I didn't want to accidentally think of what fuelled the rage inside me, of the scared looks and people crossing the street, so I tried to keep myself silent. I didn't want it to hurt anyone else.

The djinn took the stairs down three at a time and had no trouble breaking into the Toyota Celica that was parked on the street outside. He drove to Peter's house without missing a single turn, and I cursed that he had hosted a company barbeque in his backyard. I couldn't have found this place on my own, but the djinn saw all my memories as clearly as reading a book, and it knew.

The streetlamps were on and the rain hammered the metal roof of the car. It filled the cab with tinny, sporadic drumbeats and I was happy to see the lights were out in the house.

<*He's home. Don't worry. We will have revenge.* > the djinn said, and a light inside flicked on.

The door swung open and my feet led us up to the house. Without waiting to be let in, the djinn ripped the handle from the door and pushed it open.

The television turned off as Peter cried out, "Hello, is someone there?" and I was grateful he was a bachelor.

Run, Peter, you stupid fuck! Get out of here!

<Yes, Amir. Feed me rage!>

My body leapt forward, propelled by the djinn's enormous strength, and I was in the living room in front of Peter in a heartbeat.

"Amir, what are you doing here?" he said. "Get out, or I'm calling the police!"

My mouth opened and a chuckle that wasn't mine rumbled from my throat.

"Corporate said you were a liability." He stood up off the couch, his eyes white with fear. "I'd known this day was coming for months."

"What does that mean?" I said, and was surprised that my vocal chords were in my control.

"You're a sleeper agent or something, aren't you? Working with *them*."

"Are you kidding me?" I said, and I could feel the fire in my stomach, rage seeping in like poison, "Are you fucking kidding me, Peter?"

My control was removed as the djinn grabbed my ex-boss by the shirt and threw him through the wall. Dust and debris swirled as he crashed onto the tiled kitchen floor. Blood streamed from his ears and his eyes couldn't focus.

The djinn crouched over him and saw he was still breathing. He punched him in the face, and I felt the bones crunch and give way. I wish I could have looked away. I wish I could have made the djinn stop, but it only heard what it wanted to hear. I didn't want to be branded a terrorist, but I didn't want this either.

He stood me up and we left the house, the djinn's assumed task completed. I could feel myself slipping. My consciousness didn't want to stay for the ride and I had seen enough horror, but the djinn wasn't done. We walked to the car, the rain turning to steam on my skin. We got in and the engine roared to life.

< One more. One more wish and you will be released. >

Wish? You think I wish for this? For violence?

< No. I know it. It is why I chose you. >

You were wrong. I don't want this.

< You hate them, don't you? I can feel it. >

What? Who?

< The ones who stare. The ones who fear you. The ones who leave the elevator. That is truly a large wish, but I can fulfill it. >

No! No, I don't want that!

< The wish has been set, you only need to watch me now. When it is done, this vessel will be mine. >

He turned the key and headed downtown.

All I could think about was my family. They were counting on me, waiting for me to get citizenship so that they could come here. So they could be safe. Now they would never hear from me again, only see me on the news, labeled another terrorist when my body was out of my control.

I thought of my mother, and her weeping in front of her picture of Hanuman, chanting his mantra and wishing peace for me, and the car started to slow.

<What are you doing? Stop that.>

Stop what? I thought and noticed my skin had started to itch.

<Stop thinking that. Feed me your rage so I may remove this blight as you wished.>

Hanuman, he's the key. I pictured my mother again, sitting in front of her picture and chanting.

OM NAMO BHAGWATE ANJANEYAY MAHAABALAAY HANUMATE NAMAH

OM NAMO BHAGWATE ANJANEYAY MAHAABALAAY HANUMATE NAMAH

<No! Stop that!> the djinn screamed in my head, and pressed my hands to my temples, leaving the car to swerve violently.

It got control before we hit the sidewalk and slammed the car into park, holding my head as I kept my mother firmly in my mind.

OM NAMO BHAGWATE ANJANEYAY MAHAABALAAY HANUMATE NAMAH

OM NAMO BHAGWATE ANJANEYAY MAHAABALAAY HANUMATE NAMAH

<You will die, Amir! You will die with me!> it screamed, and I knew it was right. I felt my skin starting to blister, the heat was burning me from the inside out, but I the djinn losing control.

I tried to move, and was able to get the door open as cars drove by, splashing us with water. My mother kept at it inside my head.

OM NAMO BHAGWATE ANJANEYAY MAHAABALAAY HANUMATE NAMAH

OM NAMO BHAGWATE ANJANEYAY MAHAABALAAY HANUMATE NAMAH

I made it onto the sidewalk in unsure, jerky movements, and collapsed. The rain steamed when it hit my skin, hissing with each drop and creating a mist around me.

<YOU WILL BE SILENT!>

No, I told it, *I won't.*

OM NAMO BHAGWATE ANJANEYAY MAHAABALAAY HANUMATE NAMAH

My skin started to crack and blacken and I let out a scream, facing the sky and spreading my arms.

OM NAMO BHAGWATE ANJANEYAY MAHAABALAAY HANUMATE NAMAH

"You will not have me!" I'd shouted. My voice blackened and raw as a chain smoker's.

OM NAMO BHAGWATE ANJANEYAY MAHAABALAAY HANUMATE NAMAH

My skin, blistered and torn, burst into flames and I could smell it, smell my hair burn. Smell the polyester of my coat. I remember thinking, *my coat!* And grabbing out the picture of my family, throwing it away to land on the sidewalk, the edges smoldering. I collapsed beside it, my head silent except for my mother's chanting.

The rain kept falling, and the flames on my back were put out. But the damage went too deep. The djinn had burned me too deep. I felt every nerve in my body screaming, wishing for death, pleading for mercy. I heard a siren coming from a long way off as I closed my eyes, and my Mother's chanting stopped.

What Lies Beneath

———

Three days. Three fucking days we spent in that car. I don't know what possessed Amanda to buy a VW Bug. We spent three days wasting away inside its snot green shell as we headed cross country back to my pit of a hometown in Salem, New Jersey. I complain, but I really shouldn't. Amanda's an angel to stick with me after losing my job. She should've kicked my ass back to Salem and picked herself up one of those bronzed Adonis' that strutted up and down Venice Beach. But she didn't, so now she's here.

"Where do you want this box?" I asked.

Amanda sauntered in looking no worse for wear with her golden tan and bleached hair. She had the laid back attitude people associate with California. I did not. "Which box, dear?"

"The one in my hands?" I said, lifting the box of detergents and fabric softeners up.

"Take them down to the laundry room please." she said and popped onto her tiptoes to give me a peck on the cheek, then went to fetch the cat, Maurice.

My worst nightmare. I'm a dog guy, through and through, but when you love someone, you make exceptions. He wasn't a bad cat, don't get me wrong. Just ten pounds of fluff and rudeness that knew no bounds.

I went to the top of the stairs, looking down into the dark cinder block basement of doom. The steps were worn down the middle. Like it was someone's life mission to walk a hole through them. Not to mention, there was no railing. I was sure this would be how I died, and sure enough, as I took my first step forward, a grey and white ball of fluff shot in front of me. I caught the edge of his fluffy tail under my foot, but he barely slowed enough to yowl. The fur stayed and he shot into the basement.

I regained my balance and shouted "Sorry, Maurice!" but he didn't reply.

"What was that?" Amanda asked from the kitchen.

I kicked the ball of fluff off my chuck's and said, "Nothing dear!" in my best doting husband voice, then headed down the worn stairs-with-no-railing.

I surprisingly made it to the bottom without falling (first time *ever* not clutzing it up) and set the box down on the dryer. The room was small. More like a root cellar than an actual basement, with just enough room for the washer, dryer and a rusty hot water tank. "Joy of joys." I said to myself, looking at the flecking paint.

The room was dark, and no bulb hung from the ceiling, but an old flashlight sat on a nail by the water tank. I reached for it as Maurice appeared (underfoot again) and ran into a hole that led to the crawlspace under the rest of the house. I watched him dart by, and not watching myself, touched the pipe with my arm as I reached for the flashlight.

My skin hissed as it made contact, turning my wrist cherry red.

"Fuck! Goddammit, Maurice!" I clutched my wrist and stomped up the stairs. "Go to hell then, cat."

"What was that?" Amanda said, before I made it up two steps. She popped into view at the top of the stairs to block what little light was coming down.

"Maurice tried to murder me." I said, "Twice."

Amanda cocked her hip and frowned. "He's down there?"

"Yeah, he ran under my feet on the stairs, then made me burn myself when he ran into the crawlspace." I showed her my blistered wrist.

"Well, can you go get him?"

"What? Why?"

"What if there's rat poison or something down there? He could eat it and die." she said and her eyebrows drew together in the way they did when she was worried. Between that, the big eyes and her white knuckle grip on the tea towel she was holding, I knew there was no way I was coming upstairs just yet. I let out a long sigh before turning to go back down the stairs. I'd do it, but I wasn't gonna be happy about it.

I grabbed the flashlight (this time without burning myself) and crouched down on the damp floor. *Guess there's a reason it's only three hundred a month.*

I pushed the switch and the old piece of tin lit up about three feet in front of me with a wavering yellow beam. Like everything else in this house, it was a piece of shit. I remembered Amanda's worried eyes and pressed forward into that dank, dark hole.

The damp cement turned to moist gravel as I crossed the threshold. I could hear the pitter patter of rain on the other side of the wood framing, and the scuffling of Maurice digging. *Great, now he's shit down here somewhere.*

The flashlight was nearly useless, but it managed to throw enough light that I caught the reflection of Maurice's eyes. They shone in the dark for only a second before they disappeared. I army crawled closer to the corner of the space, rocks digging into my elbows and knees every inch of the way.

As I drew closer, I saw a dark shape propped up in the corner. I stopped to look at it and willed my eyes (or the flashlight) to work better in the dark. After a few seconds of squinting, I determined it wasn't the bogeyman, and crept closer.

Maurice wasn't there, but a wooden hatch opened up to reveal a dark hole leading further down.

"Not a fuckin' chance."

I peered over the edge. Rough dug walls tunneled down and I could hear the sound of dripping from below. Air blew gently from the hole, carrying up the smell of loamy decay. The ground was soft and muddy past the hard packed gravel foundation, and little paw prints led down into the tunnel.

I should have turned back, I know. I'm not brave. I don't go into creepy holes looking for cats on a regular basis, I swear (I sleep with a small night light for Christ's sake). I just couldn't shake the feeling that Maurice was going to get lost or something down there, and then Amanda would be through with me. The straw that broke the camel's back, you know? Thinking of Amanda's crinkled, worried forehead, I followed Maurice below.

The sound of water dripping got louder as I crawled deeper. The tunnel stayed narrow, with rough wooden beams framing the dirt every ten feet or so. *Who the hell built this thing?*

Maurice didn't show his stupid, fluffy face, so I kept crawling. Even when the tunnel started to narrow, I kept crawling. The flashlight started to flicker each time I set it on the ground as I army crawled, and the full extent of my stupidity struck home. *I have no idea how long this flashlight has been sitting there. The batteries could be a decade old...no wonder the thing doesn't work right.* The batteries could run out at any time, but they might last a bit longer. *She moved to this hellhole because of me, I need to find her stupid cat.*

"Maurice, come out please!" I listened, but all I heard was the dripping. "Come on, Maurice! I'm not screwin' around here. Let's get the fuck out of this hole! Wouldn't you like to go and see your–"

Mrrawwwhww

The cry echoed from behind me.

I turned around, twisting in the cramped tunnel to look behind me. *There's barely enough room to turn around down here.* I shone the light and shadows danced along the walls, glistening darkness with no cat to be seen.

"Maurice?"

I held my breath as a low rumble came from close behind. The light shook in my hand as, from behind a wood beam that cut across the ceiling, a pair of glowing eyes looked out at me.

I couldn't think, frozen to the damp ground as the chill of the tunnel sunk down into my marrow. The eyes blinked, but they didn't disappear, only watched me.

A low rumble came from the thing on the ceiling, and I tried to shuffle away from it, further down the tunnel. I didn't take my eyes off it, staring from behind the timber on the ceiling. It was an awkward crawl, but I kept going until those eyes dropped from the ceiling, landing with no sound and scurrying forward.

My heart leapt and I turned forward, crawling as fast as I could. The flashlight bounced around the tunnel, turning it into a madhouse of shadows as I barely managed to hold on in my panic. The ground dug into me deeper, rubbing my elbows, knees and hands raw. I heard another rumble, closer now, and I was sure I was a dead man.

I swung around and the eyes were close now. The flashlight showed a pale, hairless face nipping at my heels. It wasn't a human face. Not anymore. It must have been down here, waiting for someone to come. No sun had shone on its limp hair or filled its reflecting, pale blue eyes in a long time. I got the feeling that any UV on its papery skin would burn it.

It reached forward, grabbing my heel through my chuck's, its hard bony fingers gripping me with a strength they shouldn't possess as it tried to pull me closer to its open mouth. I kicked out, connecting with its snubbed nose and pushing myself off an edge I hadn't seen, falling further into darkness.

I hit the bottom of the pit, then the steel flashlight hit me, and the world went dark. Before the light was clipped, as I hit the ground, I saw a black ooze coating the wall of the pit. I felt around, and it was tacky, like tar.

I tried to move my left arm, searching for the flashlight to throw at the creature that must be crawling after me. What felt like lightning powered shards of glass shot through my elbow, and I couldn't move my fingers. I crooked the arm against me, abandoning the light and pushing with my feet until I bumped against a wall.

My mind was reeling. The darkness was absolute, and swallowed me whole. I couldn't feel my body, other than the pain in my arm and the cold seeping into me. It felt like I was watching myself in the pit. I was scrambling against the wall, eyes pinned up at the lip, switching from whimpering to screams as I waited for the pale thing to come for me.

It never did.

I don't know how long I was waiting...it felt like eternity. I ended up thinking I'd starve to death down there. No one would find me. Or would they? Surely Amanda would get worried, come look for me. She would send someone in to look for me, or come herself.

Will she though? A voice whispered.

"Hello?"

From where I'm sitting, you've solved her biggest problem.

My voice trembled and my lip quivered, "Wh-What do you mean?"

You lost your job because you were too greedy... Yes, there it is.

The blackness lit up like a nuclear explosion and the final days of my work at BGM Talent Agency flashed before my eyes. The darkness was absolute. I can't be certain if this vision was in my mind or before my eyes. I saw myself standing at the filing cabinet. The filing cabinet with the client list for BGM. I was done with them. Striking out on my own with another of the partners. I could do as much as they could. I had the talent, but they refused to see it. Refused to acknowledge my role in the company's success. So 'damn them all' had been my thought. They don't deserve me, or the talent I had brought in.

The authorities recovered the files in the trunk of my Jag a few days later. After a short court appearance, I was let off with a warning, but I was black listed in that town. No work in L.A. for criminals (not the ones that get caught anyway).

The image faded, the darkness eating it like acid, and the voice in my head returned.

Greed. It's a powerful thing. Your avarice was your downfall, and it led you here.

"Who–what are you?"

I am despair. I sit in the darkness, waiting for my next victim to stumble upon me. You have led a life of sin, Lawrence. Now I have seeped into your pores and will show you the error of your ways.

The nothing of the pit was cleaved by light as Despair split my mind open. The darkness fled as an image of me back in the office filled my vision. My assistant Melody stood before me, her perfect teeth flashing as she brushed her raven hair behind her ear. Her engagement ring shone like a beacon, but that didn't stop her from having an extra button undone. It didn't stop me from looking either. Amanda had been out of town for a month. I needed solace, I needed release. Melody wasn't anything, and she was let go soon after. But she was there, and I wanted her, so I took her. She didn't complain, and Amanda didn't find out...no harm no foul.

No harm?

"I didn't say–"

I am inside of you, Lawrence. You spoke it with your heart. I do not need your lips to admit the blackness that is in your soul.

I shifted, staring at nothing and seeing Melody straddling my lap. It was so real...I thought I could feel her weight on me, pressing on my thighs. But it was only a vision, it wasn't real. *Then what is touching me?*

I heard a rumble coming from in front of me and my eyes focused, coming back to reality and leaving me in the dark again. Even in that horrid nothingness, I could see the faint outline of something sitting on my legs. The rumble came again, and my skin chilled. I felt my pants warm as the thing on my lap shifted, coming closer. It's horrid breath filled my nostrils and I gagged, lifting my good arm to cover my nose.

Bony fingers clasped my wrist, and pulled my hand down to my side. My other arm hung useless, and my heart felt like it had lost synchronicity as my mind was rent with fear.

I have fed, my love. Now is your turn. Despair said, but I knew it wasn't talking to me.

The creature drew closer still, smelling my neck and running a slimy, smooth tongue along my skin. I shuddered and began to cry, my body shaking as the creature breathed deeper. Like it was absorbing my fear.

"P-please." I said, but it didn't let me finish begging for my life.

Boney fingers crept into my mouth, filling it with dirt and the black ooze that coated the pit. I gagged as the finger pressed down my tongue and filled my throat. I bucked, and tried to get the thing off me, but it was useless. It was small, but immovable with a strength that belied its size. Tears streamed down my face as it pushed its fingers deeper. I gagged and choked and wished it would stop. I wished it had killed me quickly, as snot poured out of my nose. I couldn't wail, or cry or plead for my life. Only gag as the darkness shoved fear down my throat.

I don't know exactly when I died... but I remember there was no burst of light or angelic song. The main thing I noticed was the pain was gone. I suddenly felt like I could breathe. The weight from my lap and the hand that held my arm to my side were gone. So was the pain from my elbow.

The darkness went on forever, and I waited there (having no other choice). I don't know if an hour or a decade passed...nothing was clear in the black in-between from life to afterlife. I thought of what Despair had said. Remembered too vividly what the creature Fear had done. I'm glad that I was unable to sleep, or didn't seem to be anyway (for all I know, it was all sleep though my eyes felt open). I was thankful for the stillness and the calm that came with knowing that nothing would happen in that place. I don't know how I knew that, but it seemed true while I was there. But now I'm no longer there, and calm is a memory.

As I laid in the dark, a pin-prick of light appeared in the distance. I squinted, trying to see what it was, but it was drawing closer fast. It grew, and I saw the light was pouring out from a doorway behind a figure in a black, hooded robe.

Surely this is a joke? Death is in a robe?

Cliche or not, the robed figure reached out to me, not with a sickle, but a shepherd's crook.

"Wait! I'm not ready!" I said, but the robed figure paid no heed. They caught me around the waist with their crook and pulled me into the light.

I fell to the floor, all sensation returning to my body as my hands and knees slapped onto the tiles. My lungs were suddenly useful and I drew in my first new breath with a gasp that sent me into a coughing fit.

I looked up as my breathing returned to normal and a small man with receding hair and thick glasses stood before me. He pushed the frames up with the eraser of a pencil and looked at his clipboard.

"Lawrence Waits?" he asked.

"Uh...yeah. That's me." I said, straightening.

He snapped and another small man appeared at his side, handing me an orange linen robe.

"Please follow me, Lawrence." the little bespectacled man said, "Judgment awaits."

Judgment

This is where we depart from our dearly departed. They now stand trial for their transgressions. I would have you know that I felt, like most of you likely feel, that these people had been through enough torment.

They waited in the void until assigned their judge. Then, pulled from the darkness, they were brought to this room of carved Honduran rosewood and gold filigree. A large door with intricate, swirling carvings sat to my right. The defendants sat across from me in a small stand of benches arranged by the colour of their robe (something Phanuel began when he complained, 'all humans look alike'). A podium stood between us. To my left, and to the left of the judge's bench, was an open pit that led to hell. Flecks of soot and the stench of sulfur wafted from it in pulsing clouds. The defendant's eyes darted toward it every couple of minutes as they wrung their hands and waited to begin.

I sat by in this nearly empty courtroom behind a small desk. Only myself, the judge, and the shadow creatures who acted as bailiffs were present. I watched as the judge jotted down his notes while the humans recounted the stories of their final hours. I felt a knot in my stomach as I thought about the single word he was likely scrawling on each file. *Guilty.*

Our Honorable Judge Phanuel has had a bad couple of centuries. He was assigned the court of America, and the fires burned hotter ever since. Personally, I don't see what all the fuss is about. It should be our policy as angels to turn the other cheek. To forgive the human souls and allow them to go to heaven even if they might have stolen a bag of Doritos from time to time. But what do I know? I'm just a clerk. A witness to the proceedings.

Today, we have a group of seven sinners who have been accused of rubbing elbows with the supernatural. After hearing their stories, I have no doubt that they did. As these cases go, where a human life meets its end at the hands of a supernatural being, they can't be condemned on that alone. They have to have *wanted* to interact with them and to have caused harm by doing so. From the quick notes Phanuel made, I feared for these souls. Since being assigned clerk duties (a demotion for my meddling with Abraham), I have only been able to witness.

"I would first like to review the case of Alex Rodrigo." Phanuel said, looking over his half moon glasses.

A medium built man with black hair stepped forward and took his place at the podium before Phanuel, adjusting his glasses and chewing his lip.

"Here, your...honor? Your grace?" Alex said.

Phanuel looked down his pointed nose at Alex and a snarl played with his upper lip. He didn't answer, but tapped his notes and said, "You have been found guilty of fraternizing with a supernatural being. But, you must be found guilty of *more,* as we stated when you all arrived."

Alex looked at the floor and his glasses slid forward. He pushed them back up his nose. "I understand."

"On the second charge, I find you guilty of one of the most vile sins,"

Great. Not this again. I sat back against the hard oak bench, rubbing the back of my neck.

"I find you guilty of Envy." Phanuel said.

"What?" Alex said, looking at his peers who awaited judgment. "How can I be found guilty of envy?"

"You were envious of the man who took your place at the marketing firm. You were envious of Mike when his ticket won, and you took his life. You, Alex, caused irreparable harm to him and his family through your envy."

A slippery form moved from the shadows, its empty eye sockets staring. "Time to go, human." it said, and wrapped its cracked charcoal fingers around Alex's arm.

His sleeve started to smolder and his eyes bugged. Another creature came from the shadows, grabbing Alex's other arm as he thrashed, trying to escape.

"This is bullshit! I didn't ask for this! I never wanted to hurt Mike!"

He made one final thrash, and for a moment I thought he was going to shake loose from the shadows that gripped him. The shadow on his left ended that by launching an elbow into his ribs, knocking the air from his lungs.

Alex's glasses fell to the floor. They clattered on the polished marble as the shadows dragged him toward the hell mouth. They threw him into the opening and he disappeared with a puff of smoke and a scream.

The other mortals looked on in horror, but they had no time to speak, no time to react.

"Next, I will have Amir come to the stand." Phanuel said, motioning to a fellow clerk who wheeled in a tray of tea and biscuits. The clerk (a much smaller, more cherub specimen than myself) winged over a tray and placed it before Phanuel as Amir took the stand.

Eyes blank and jaw tight, he rubbed his arms like he was feeling the flesh underneath. Making sure it was still there. His curly black hair hung in his face, and his lips were near chalk white.

"Amir Kaur." Phanuel took a sip of the tea, "You are guilty of consorting with the supernatural, and a powerful evil at that."

"I do not protest this charge." Amir said, keeping his eyes on the floor, still rubbing his arms.

"Good. You really don't have a choice." Phanuel leaned back in his chair. "I am also charging you with wrath."

Amir closed his eyes and bowed his head further, his lips moving silently.

"Your wrath nearly burned down a city." Phanuel continued. "Had it not gone unchecked, who knows how much damage the djinn would have wrought?"

Amir looked up, eyes meeting Phanuel's. "I agree."

Phanuel smiled and rubbed cookie crumbs from his fingers before picking up the gavel. "Then I sentence you to–"

The door to the court swung open and a blast of light filled the room. A tall, lanky man came through the blazing white. The door slammed behind him and he glowered at Phanuel, his round face tight around the eyes. Tawny hair covered his entire body, and he carried a wooden staff that was as tall as he was. He switched it from his left to right hand before pointing it at Phanuel. "You do not have jurisdiction over this man's soul."

"And who the hell are you supposed to be?" Phanuel said, shooting to his feet so hard his chair fell back.

"I am Hanuman, the Monkey King to you, and Amir is mine." he smiled, showing sharp canines. He held his staff pointed at the bench with the steadiness of a surgeon.

Phanuel's face twisted. His thin, pale lips lifted into a snarl. That was normal. I had seen that a million times over the last eon. The glint in his eyes though, that was new.

"Amir is in *my* courtroom, and you can not come in here–"

"This man died with my chant on his lips, he is mine. Besides, who will stop me?" Hanuman said, lowering his staff and tucking the long fingers of his left hand into his red jacket. "You?"

"Guards!" Phanuel shouted and I ducked behind my meager desk for cover.

Two of the shadow reapers came forward from dark corners of the room, but Hanuman was ready. He plucked two hairs from his chest and blew them toward his attackers. They grew in the air so fast that, had I been any lesser being, I wouldn't have seen them change at all.

The copies of Hanuman were ready even as they took form. They spread their feet and met the oncoming shadows with their staffs. Carbon copied muscles strained, and with an easy brutality, the clones dispatched the shadowy bailiffs.

"Amir comes with me," Hanuman said, his eyes cold and black and bottomless, "you have no right to his soul."

Phanuel's mouth hung open. He'd risked all out war by sending the shadows after Hanuman. All the Monkey King had to do now was cry out, and the other pantheons would descend on the courtroom to ask for Phanuel's head. It had happened before, and it would happen now. What was the price of one angel in comparison with the bloodshed of a war between Gods?

Red crept up Phanuel's normally alabaster throat and his eyes bulged. "Get him out of my sight!" He spat.

Hanuman bowed. The clones moved forward, flanking Amir and herding him to the exit. He rose and looked at Phanuel one more time, a smile playing at his lips. "Fare thee well, angel." he said before turning and following the trio out the doors.

"Wow." I said, unable to help myself. I hadn't seen action like that in a millennia. Two shadows dispatched before my eyes! And by the Monkey King himself!

Phanuel glowered down at me and I looked back to my empty notepad, trying to appear busy.

"We will have a short recess. Reconvene in one half hour." he said, and stormed from the bench to his chambers.

The shadows left their posts and the accused shifted in their seats. They looked worried, and I didn't blame them. Who knew what would happen now? Surely hell was on the table before, but now that one had escaped 'justice', I was sure Phanuel would burn them all.

A teen boy with shaggy brown hair, and more acne than one would think a dead person could possess, stood from his seat on the wooden bench. I watched him, curious at his lackadaisical attitude. He stretched, and wiped his hands on his yellow robe while smacking his lips. Had he been sleeping? I checked the files I had for the trial. *Yellow robe; that's Adrian.*

"Hey," he said, "what happened to the pale dude?"

"He went to his chambers." I said, then clasped my hands over my mouth. "I'm sorry, I'm not to intervene." I looked away. This was shaping up to be an odd trial indeed.

Adrian tapped a man in an orange robe, (Lawrence) and he shimmied past him and onto the floor. He walked to the bench, which stood at his eye level, and reached a lanky arm across to snatch up the files from the desk.

"What in heaven are you doing?" I asked.

Adrian looked up at me and blinked slowly. "Don't have a cow. I'm just lookin' to see who's next."

He went back to looking through the files, shuffling through them until the door behind the bench opened with a creak of hinges.

"Get back here you idiot!" the girl in blue (Ruby) hissed between her teeth.

Adrian slipped the files back onto the desk as Phanuel turned to beckon his minions. He slid around Lawrence, who had leaned back enough for him to pass, and sat down as Phanuel's snarling visage popped up behind the bench.

"Right, where were we?" he said. His typical, holier than thou attitude returned. There was one less shadow guard that slunk into the court behind him.

He looked through the files, and I felt a bead of sweat roll down my forehead. I rubbed my eye when it found its target, but barely noticed the sting.

If Adrian had changed the order of the files with his meddling, Phanuel didn't seem to notice. He pulled the next file even as Adrian whispered to the woman in Indigo. He did a poor job of hiding the whisper, but he needn't have bothered. He could have spoken freely. There were no rules about collusion. Though, how could they have known?

"Indigo," Phanuel said, "step to the podium."

Lydia stood, her head bowed and brow furrowed. She had a look of... determination? Or like she was thinking hard about what Adrian had said. What had he seen in those files?

"Lydia Cole." Phanuel said, and she looked up at him, "You are charged with one count of fraternizing with a supernatural being–"

"Not guilty." Lydia said.

"Excuse me?" Phanuel stammered, drawing back into his chair like she'd spit venom.

"You were going to ask how I plead, right?" she said, staring up at him with ferocious eyes. "I plead, *not guilty*."

He looked at the file, then back to Lydia. "You were killed by a minion of hell, woman. How much more plain can it be?"

"Yes. I was killed by a hellhound. But I didn't do much fraternizing." her lip curled and she rubbed her neck.

"What would you call it then?"

"Murder."

Phanuel blinked. He looked at his file and back at her again. "You sold your soul."

"I did. To a man. Not to a demon, a genie, or whatever the fuck killed poor Alex. He was a man. If you want to charge someone, charge him."

Phanuel's eyes went cold. "Don't worry, he'll get his turn."

"So I bartered for something that I had no proof existed. I was lured there by a man who used magical cologne and made big promises. I was stupid, but he was a man. Not a 'supernatural being.'"

"Be that as it may," Phanuel relaxed in his chair, "you have another charge against you. You are also charged with–"

"Greed?" she said.

Phanuel stiffened, and the file in his hand crumpled. "Yes. Greed." He glared at me, and I sat stock still, hoping the sweat beading my face didn't give me away. I was starting to like this batch of humans.

"If wanting my son to live another day means I committed the sin of greed, then I can live with that." she paused and then waved as she said, "Or die with that, or whatever."

"And die you did. You are so judged and you will spend eternity in the flames."

Ruby stood from her place on the defendant's bench as the gavel lifted. "Wait! You said that one charge alone wasn't enough to condemn us to hell. You said so yourself; we need two charges levied against us."

Phanuel's lips puckered into a small and silent *O*. He laid the gavel down and rubbed his temples while Lydia stared daggers at him.

He picked up the gavel and brought it down again in a single, swift motion. "You are pardoned for your singular sin. Get out of my sight." he said, and the door Hanuman took Amir through opened to blind us again.

Lydia wasted no time and bolted for the door before any sinister, shadowy hands could take hold of her. The doors slammed shut behind her as she cleared the jamb. I was surprised her heel wasn't caught in it.

Amazing. In all the time I have been witnessing, I have never seen such a ruling. What information lies in Phanuel's files? If a glance from a lanky teen drew enough information to earn Lydia a pardon, what else was in there?

I looked at the copy of my files. All they contained were the defendants names, the date and means of death along with their corresponding robe colors.

Adrian was already whispering to the girl in blue.

"Next to the stand is Ruby White." Phanuel said.

Ruby pushed Adrian away and picked up the hem of her blue robe. She slid off the bench and made her way to the podium. The others had looked scared or, in Lydia's case, angry, but not her. Her small round face remained placid as a glacier, unmoved by the events of the trial so far.

She stood at the podium and set her hands on its flat top. She looked up at Phanuel and said, "List my crimes, monster."

He set Ruby's file down and raised his eyebrow. He looked at her for a moment, as if he wasn't sure what to make of this human. "Consorting with–"

"Bullshit. Again."

"Excuse me?"

"You *just* let Lydia walk into heaven, and she struck a deal with a witch doctor. I made no deal. I was promised nothing, and gave nothing." she raised a hand at the others waiting judgment, "Neither did they. So what's this *really* about, huh?"

Crimson started to creep up Phanuel's neck. He looked around the courtroom, eyes flashing wildly. It was as though he expected to find some secret conspirator in a corner with a recording device.

"This is about you, and your *sin*!" he spat, darting forward in his chair and pointing down at her. "You are touched by wickedness, and paid the price for it with your demise–"

"What wickedness, exactly?"

"Your, well, your..." he looked down at his paper, his authority crumbling by the second as his cronies watched from their dark corners, "pride. Your pride was your downfall, and this is a mortal sin."

"I think you're making a mockery of this court, monster. I talked to these people while we waited for this farce to begin." Ruby said, "I talked to Alex. Did *you*?"

Phanuel stared at her, his jaw clenched tight. In the silence, I could hear his teeth grinding. I looked to his shadows, worried about some secret call button that would have them sweep Ruby away.

"I did." she repeated. "He was kind, and sweet. I talked to him when I was alive, on the night I died. He wasn't evil. He wasn't a man who lived enviously. Who the hell hasn't been envious? You found a moment of weakness and you exploited a system that would allow you to throw him into hell without a second thought."

"You dare—"

"You are the one who dares!" Ruby said. "You're taking the souls of innocents, souls of people broken by these supernatural creatures, and throwing us into a pit for eternity. For what?"

Ruby was captivating. She was small, like me, but she wasn't backing down from Phanuel's stare (a stare that made my guts turn into snakes every day). How did she do that? I didn't know then. I still don't know how or why I felt that stirring inside me.

"I've had enough of your impudence," Phanuel said, "take her below." he waved at Ruby and his shadows stepped forward.

Sweat was pouring down my face, and my lips were numb. My body started to move, but I don't remember asking it to. I floated toward Ruby as if I was in a dream, leaving my meager notes for the trial behind and flying over my desk. Time had slowed. Ruby closed her eyes, waiting for the shadows to clutch at her with bony fingers. Instead, I placed my hand on her shoulder.

She turned, looked me in the eye, and gave me a warm smile. "I thought you couldn't intervene?"

"I really don't know what's come over me." I said.

The shadows drew near and I stepped in front of Ruby, shielding her from their touch.

"Zadkiel, what in heaven are you doing?" Phanuel shouted, stepping out from behind his desk.

Adrian, Lawrence, Tiffany and Ruby. They were depending on me to make this right. I needed to stop this charade.

"I have watched you sentence humans for two centuries, Brother." I said. "You have not shown mercy to a single soul, and you would throw these humans into the pit as well."

"What business is that of yours? You are a clerk, not a judge. You take notes, I cast judgment for God!"

"I had thought so too, but now I'm not sure." I said, "Ruby and Lydia made excellent points. I will tell you now that Adrian looked at your files while you were in your chambers." Phanuel's head snapped toward the defendants. Tiffany and Lawrence jumped while Adrian chuckled and shrugged his shoulders. "After only minutes reading those files, he found ways to dismiss these cases that you have built for them."

Phanuel looked back at me and snarled, "So what?"

"So what?" I wiped my brow with my sleeve, "So you have been damning people for some other reason than Father's judgment."

The shadows began to withdraw, and I knew this was true.

"How long, Phanuel?" I said, "How long have you been working with Lucifer?"

"You have no idea." Phanuel said. "No idea what I have been through to get to where I am now. They are humans! Not worthy of the eternal city, and not worthy of Father's love!"

I hung my head, shame washing over me in waves. "If you could only see yourself." I walked up to him and placed my narrow hand on his shoulder. "Repent, Brother, and I will ask Father for mercy. I am as guilty as you are in all this. I should have seen it sooner."

"Repent?" he pushed my arm away. "Repent? I would rather burn."

I shook my head and sorrow filled my heart. I walked past him and took the seat behind the bench as Phanuel sneered at me. "Phanuel, angel of heaven, I find you guilty of consorting with the Devil. You are also guilty of Greed, Pride and Wrath. I sentence you to hell."

"Fuck yourself, you arrogant little prick." Phanuel spat. "My shadows cannot act against me." he said, and they stayed tucked away in the corners.

"They are no longer yours," I said, and pointed to him with the gavel. "And they won't be taking you."

The door at the back of the courtroom shuddered, and banged open to flood the court with light.

"Close your eyes!" I shouted to the humans, and hoped they wouldn't peek.

A vaguely human form entered the room on a torrent of wind. Phanuel screamed as it descended upon him. A million piercing blue eyes dotted its chalk white skin, all staring at the judge. The archangel's wings protruded from awkward, backward jointed limbs. Long, gnarled fingers reached out, clawing at Phanuel.

"No! I did nothing!" Phanuel screamed, "It was Lucifer! He tricked me!"

The archangel paid no heed and grasped Phanuel's throat. It screeched, and the spectacle cracked over my eye. It lifted Phanuel in the air and carried him to the hell mouth.

"Wait!" I shouted over the wind buffeting the room from its insane wings. "Bring Alex Rodrigo back. He did not receive a fair trial."

The room shook as the angel said, "I shall." then disappeared into the mouth."

The room was still for a moment, and I could hear the human's panting, crouched behind the defendant's bench.

"Stay where you are, and keep down. Michael won't be long." I said.

A second after I spoke, the room shook again. Michael swept through the court and out the doors that lead into heaven. The great doors swung shut behind him, leaving us alone; half blind and rattled.

"What the fuck?" Lawrence said, rising to his feet. "What the FUCK?"

"Whoa, was that an angel?" Adrian said.

"Yes, a very powerful one." I said.

"Are you all like that?" Tiffany said, "Like, underneath?"

I shrugged, "Sort of."

"Alex!" Ruby shouted and ran toward the lump of clothes that held a man on the floor. She knelt beside him and gently turned him toward her. A lidless eye steamed in the socket as it re-grew. The right side of his face knitted itself back together, repairing before our eyes, and Alex's ground beef complexion slowly returned to its previous caramel coloring.

The others came over on shaky legs, skin pale against their brightly colored robes.

"Wha–what happens now?" Tiffany said. She shivered and began to rub her arms as if the chill on her skin was an issue of warmth.

"I will take Phanuel's place." I said, and raised the gavel. My arm vibrated as the power of the gavel radiated up to my elbow. Phanuel's files laid before me, and I thumbed through them quickly.

Tiffany was wayward with love, but saying she died from her lust or caused harm to others was ridiculous. Alex, like Ruby said, wasn't more envious than any would be in his situation. Ruby was hard headed, and probably should have gone with the love of her life, but to say that's what killed her is insane.

Adrian was a sloth, no doubt there, but he was bright and would have contributed to society (even if it was the bare minimum).

Lawrence. He lived a bad life. He did bad things, and certainly lived with an insatiable appetite for success. Had he not met Fear and Despair in the pit, would he have turned it around for Amanda? It's hard to say. She knew about the affair, though she never told him. She knew about the blacklisting and his theft of the client files, and she stayed with him. She'd moved across the country when she didn't need to. If she could forgive him, then what right did I have to deny him paradise?

The gavel sang in my hand and I knew it held the power to do the right thing, regardless of what Phanuel had done.

"Tiffany Hebert, Ruby White, Adrian DeGlass, Alex Rodrigo and Lawrence Waits." I looked down at them and they stood there with fear and hope fighting to control their faces. "I pronounce you all free to enter heaven." I said, and brought the gavel down hard.

A collective sigh of relief rippled through the defendants. Adrian hugged Ruby then shook Lawrence's shoulder. Tiffany covered her eyes and began to sob.

The doors opened. The five humans left walked toward them with Lawrence and Adrian helping Alex as he limped along.

They passed into the white light and the doors slammed closed behind them. The day was over, and I sat in a new seat. The lights flickered and the shadows grew in the room as I sat there, replaying the events of the trial. I looked down at the small desk where I had sat for centuries. I sat there as scores of humans were sent to hell. All because Phanuel received favors from Lucifer, and not because of the weight of their crimes.

I leaned back in the chair and made a vow to myself, and to whatever shadow creatures remained listening.

"I will judge fairly. I owe that to all of you who came before. For all the days when I said nothing."

The room remained silent. No ghosts were there to haunt me or to tell me it wouldn't outweigh the debt on my own soul (if I had one). I sighed to that empty courtroom and lifted the gavel again, pointed to a shadow and said, "Bring in the next group."

The End

About the Publisher

Heorot Press was founded in 2023 as a publishing banner for author E.B. Hunter's works.

Read more at https://ebhunterauthor.ca.

Milton Keynes UK
Ingram Content Group UK Ltd.
UKHW010705220124
436466UK00007B/329